Billionaire
Boy

David Walliams

Billionaire
Boy

Illustrated by Tony Ross

HarperCollins *Children's Books*

First published in paperback in Great Britain by HarperCollins *Children's Books* 2011
HarperCollins *Children's Books* is a division of HarperCollins*Publishers* Ltd
77–85 Fulham Palace Road, Hammersmith, London W6 8JB

The HarperCollins *Children's Books* website address is
www.harpercollins.co.uk

28

Text © David Walliams 2010
Illustrations © Tony Ross 2010

David Walliams and Tony Ross assert the moral right to be identified
as the author and illustrator of this work

ISBN 978-0-00-737108-2

Printed and bound in England by
Clays Ltd, St Ives plc

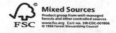

Mixed Sources
Product group from well-managed
forests and other controlled sources
www.fsc.org Cert no. SW-COC-001806
© 1996 Forest Stewardship Council

FSC is a non-profit international organisation established to promote the
responsible management of the world's forests. Products carrying the FSC
label are independently certified to assure consumers that they come
from forests that are managed to meet the social, economic and
ecological needs of present and future generations.

Find out more about HarperCollins and the environment at
www.harpercollins.co.uk/green

Voor Lara,

Ik hou meer van je, dan ik met woorden kan zeggen

Also by David Walliams

The Boy in the Dress
Mr Stink
Gangsta Granny
Ratburger

Thank yous:

I would like to thank a few people who helped make this book possible. I did most of the hard work, but I have to mention them. First, Tony Ross, for his illustrations. He could have coloured them in, but apparently you have to pay him extra. Next, I would like to thank Ann-Janine Murtagh. She is in charge of all HarperCollins children's books and is very nice and always has great suggestions. I have to say that, she is the boss. Then there is Nick Lake who is my editor. His job is to help me with the characters and story, and I couldn't do it without him. Well, I could actually, but he would cry if he wasn't mentioned here.

The cover was designed by James Stevens, and the interior was designed by Elorine Grant. I could say that 'Elorine' is a silly name, but I won't, that would be cruel. The publicist is Sam White. If you see me on *Loose Women* trying to flog this book, don't blame me, blame her. Sarah Benton, thank you so much for being the most wonderful marketing manager, whatever that is. The sales directors Kate Manning and Victoria Boodle did something too, though I am not sure what. Thank you also to the copyeditor Lily Morgan and the proofreader Rosalind Turner. If there are any spelling mistakes it's their fault. And thank you to my agent Paul Stevens at Independent for taking 10% plus VAT of my fee for sitting in his office all day drinking tea and eating biscuits.

Of course, a big thank you to *you* for buying this book. Really you shouldn't be bothering reading this bit though. It's boring. You need to get on with reading the story. It has already been called 'one of the greatest stories ever written'. Thanks for that, Mum.

1

Meet Joe Spud

Have you ever wondered what it would be like to have a million pounds?

Or a billion?

How about a trillion?

Or even a gazillion?

Meet Joe Spud.

Joe didn't *have* to imagine what it would be like to have loads and loads and loads of money. He was only twelve, but he was ridiculously, preposterously rich.

Joe had everything he could ever want.

- 100-inch plasma widescreen flat-screen high-definition TV in every room in the house ✓
- 500 pairs of Nike trainers ✓
- A grand-prix race track in the back garden ✓
- A robot dog from Japan ✓
- A golf buggy with the number plate 'SPUD 2' to drive around the grounds of his house ✓
- A waterslide which went from his

bedroom into an indoor Olympic-sized swimming pool ✔

- Every computer game in the world ✔
- 3-D IMAX cinema in the basement ✔
- A crocodile ✔
- 24-hour personal masseuse ✔
- Underground 10-lane bowling alley ✔
- Snooker table ✔
- Popcorn dispenser ✔
- Skateboard park ✔
- Another crocodile ✔
- £100,000 a week pocket money ✔
- A rollercoaster in the back garden ✔
- A professional recording studio in the attic ✔
- Personalised football coaching from the England team ✔
- A real-life shark in a tank ✔

In short, Joe was one horribly spoilt kid. He went to a ridiculously posh school. He flew on private planes whenever he went on holiday. Once, he even had Disneyworld closed for the day, just so he wouldn't have to queue for any rides.

Here's Joe. Speeding around his own private racetrack in his own Formula One racing car.

Some very rich children have miniature

versions of cars specially built for them. Joe wasn't one of those children. Joe needed his Formula One car made a bit *bigger*. He was quite fat, you see. Well, you would be, wouldn't you? If you could buy all the chocolate in the world.

You will have noticed that Joe is on his own in that picture. To tell the truth, speeding around a racetrack isn't that much fun when you are on

your own, even if you do have a squillion pounds. You really need someone to race against. The problem was Joe didn't have any friends. Not one.

- Friends ✕

Now, driving a Formula One car and unwrapping a king-size Mars Bar are two things you shouldn't try and do at the same time. But it had been a few moments since Joe had last eaten and he was hungry. As he entered the chicane, he tore open the wrapper with his teeth and took a bite of the delicious chocolate-coated nougat and caramel. Unfortunately, Joe only had one hand on the steering wheel, and as the wheels of the car hit the verge, he lost control.

The multi-million-pound Formula One car careered off the track, span around, and hit a tree.

SSSSSSSSSCCCCCCCC CCCCCCCCCRRRRRRRRR RRRRRREEEEEEEEEEEEEEECC CCCCCCCCCCHHHHH HHHHHH!!!!!!!!!!!!!!! !!!!!!!!!!!!!!!!!!!!!!!!!!!!!!!

The tree was unharmed. But the car was a write-off. Joe squeezed himself out of the cockpit. Luckily Joe wasn't hurt, but he was a little dazed, and he tottered back to the house.

"Dad, I crashed the car," said Joe as he entered the palatial living room.

Mr Spud was short and fat, just like his son. Hairier in a lot of places too, apart from his head – which was bald and shiny. Joe's dad was sitting on a hundred-seater crocodile skin sofa and didn't look up from reading that day's copy of the *Sun*.

"Don't worry Joe," he said. "I'll buy you another one."

Joe slumped down on the sofa next to his dad.

"Oh, happy birthday, by the way, Joe." Mr Spud handed an envelope to his son, without taking his eyes off the girl on Page 3.

Joe opened the envelope eagerly. How much money was he going to receive this year? The card, which read 'Happy 12th Birthday Son', was quickly discarded in favour of the cheque inside.

Joe could barely disguise his disappointment. "One million pounds?" he scoffed. "Is that all?"

"What's the matter, son?" Mr Spud put down his newspaper for a moment.

"You gave me a million *last* year," whined Joe. "When I turned eleven. Surely I should get more now I'm twelve?"

Mr Spud reached into the pocket of his shiny grey designer suit and pulled out his chequebook. His suit was horrible, and horribly expensive. "I'm so sorry son," he said. "Let's make it two million."

Now, it's important you realise that Mr Spud had not always been this rich.

Not so long ago the Spud family had lived a very humble life. From the age of sixteen, Mr Spud worked in a vast loo-roll factory on the outskirts of town. Mr Spud's job at the factory was *sooooo* boring. He had to roll the paper around the cardboard inner tube.

Roll after roll.

Day after day.

Year after year.

Decade after decade.

This he did, over and over again, until nearly all his hope had gone. He would stand all day by the conveyer belt with hundreds of other bored workers, repeating the same mind-numbing task.

Every time the paper was rolled onto one cardboard tube, the whole thing started again. And every loo roll was the same. Because the family was so poor, Mr Spud used to make birthday and Christmas presents for his son from the loo roll inner tubes. Mr Spud never had enough money to buy Joe all the latest toys, but would make him something like a loo-roll racing car, or a loo-roll fort complete with dozens of loo-roll soldiers. Most of them got broken and ended up in the bin. Joe did manage to save a sad looking little loo-roll space rocket, though he wasn't sure why.

The only good thing about working in a factory was that Mr Spud had lots of time to daydream. One day he had a daydream that was to revolutionise bottom wiping forever.

Why not invent a loo roll that is moist on one side and dry on the other? he thought, as he

rolled paper around his thousandth roll of the day. Mr Spud kept his idea top-secret and toiled for hours locked in the bathroom of their little council flat getting his new double-sided loo roll exactly right.

When Mr Spud finally launched 'Bumfresh', it was an instant phenomenon. Mr Spud sold a billion rolls around the world every day. And every time a roll was sold, he made 10p. It all added up to an awful lot of money, as this simple maths equation shows.

10p x 1,000,000,000 rolls x 365 days a year = a lot of wonga.

Joe Spud was only eight at the time 'Bumfresh' was launched, and his life was turned upside down in a heartbeat. First, Joe's mum and dad split up. It turned out that for many years Joe's mum Carol had been having a torrid affair with Joe's Cub Scout leader, Alan. She took a ten billion pound divorce settlement; Alan swapped his canoe for a gigantic yacht. Last anyone had heard, Carol and Alan were sailing off the coast of Dubai, pouring vintage champagne on their Crunchy Nut Cornflakes every morning. Joe's dad seemed to get over the split quickly and began going on dates with an endless parade of Page 3 girls.

Soon father and son moved out of their poky council flat and into an enormous stately home. Mr Spud named it 'Bumfresh Towers'.

The house was so large it was visible from outer space. It took five minutes just to motor up the drive. Hundreds of newly-planted, hopeful little trees lined the mile-long gravel track. The house had seven kitchens, twelve sitting rooms, forty-seven bedrooms and eighty-nine bathrooms.

Even the bathrooms had en-suite bathrooms. And some of those en-suite bathrooms had en-en-suite bathrooms.

Despite living there for a few years, Joe had probably only ever explored around a quarter of the main house. In the endless grounds were tennis courts, a boating lake, a helipad and even a 100m ski-slope complete with mountains of fake snow. All the taps, door handles and even toilet seats were solid gold. The carpets were made from mink fur, he and his dad drank orange squash from priceless antique medieval goblets, and for a while they had a butler called Otis who was also an orang-utan. But he had to be given the sack.

"Can I have a *proper* present as well, Dad?" said Joe, as he put the cheque in his trouser pocket. "I mean, I've got loads of money already."

"Tell me what you want, son, and I'll get one of my assistants to buy it," said Mr Spud. "Some solid gold sunglasses? I've got a pair. You can't see out of 'em but they are very expensive."

Joe yawned.

"Your own speedboat?" ventured Mr Spud.

Joe rolled his eyes. "I've got two of those. Remember?"

"Sorry, son. How about a quarter of a million pounds worth of WHSmith vouchers?"

"Boring! Boring! Boring!" Joe stamped his feet in frustration. Here was a boy with high-class problems.

Mr Spud looked forlorn. He wasn't sure there was anything left in the world that he could buy his only child. "Then what, son?"

Joe suddenly had a thought. He pictured himself going round the racetrack all on his own, racing against himself. "Well, there is something I really want…" he said, tentatively.

"Name it, son," said Mr Spud.

"A friend."

2

Bum Boy

"Bum boy," said Joe.

"*Bum Boy*?" spluttered Mr Spud. "What else do they call you at school, son?"

"The Bog Roll Kid..."

Mr Spud shook his head in disbelief. He had sent his son to the most expensive school in England. St Cuthbert's School for Boys. The fees were £200,000 a term and all the boys had to wear Elizabethan ruffs and tights. Here is a picture of Joe in his school uniform. He looks a bit silly, doesn't he?

So the last thing that Mr Spud expected was

that his son would get bullied. Bullying was something that happened to poor people. But the truth was that Joe had been picked on ever since he started at the school. The posh kids hated him, because his dad had made his money out of loo rolls. They said that was 'awfully vulgar'.

"Bottom Billionaire, The Bum-Wipe Heir, Master Plop-Paper," continued Joe. "And that's just the teachers."

Most of the boys at Joe's school were Princes, or at least Dukes or Earls. Their families had made their fortunes from owning lots of land. That made them 'old money'. Joe had quickly come to learn that money was only worth having if it was old. New money from selling loo rolls didn't count.

The posh boys at St Cuthbert's had names like Nathaniel Septimus Ernest Bertram Lysander Tybalt Zacharias Edmund Alexander Humphrey Percy Quentin Tristan Augustus Bartholomew Tarquin Imogen Sebastian Theodore Clarence Smythe.

That was just one boy.

The subjects were all ridiculously posh too. This was Joe's school timetable:

Monday

Latin

Straw Hat wearing

Royal studies

The study of etiquette

Show-jumping

Ballroom dancing

Debating Society ('This house believes that it is vulgar to do up the bottom button on your waistcoat')

Scone eating

Bow-tie tying

Punting

Polo (the sport with horses and sticks, not the mint)

Tuesday

Ancient Greek

Croquet

Pheasant shooting

Being beastly to servants class

Mandolin level 3

History of Tweed

Nose in the air hour

Learning to step over the homeless person as
you leave the opera

Finding your way out of a maze

Wednesday

Fox-hunting

Flower arranging

Conversing about the weather

History of cricket

History of the brogue

Playing Stately Home Top Trumps

Reading *Harper's Bazaar*

Ballet appreciation class

Top-hat polishing

Fencing (the one with swords, not selling
stolen goods)

Thursday

Antique furniture appreciation hour

Range Rover tyre changing class

Discussion of whose daddy is the richest

Competition to see who is best friends with
Prince Harry

Learning to talk posh

Rowing club

Debating Society ('This house believes that
muffins are best toasted')

Chess

The study of coats of arms

A lecture on how to talk loudly in restaurants

Friday

Poetry reading (Mcdieval English)

History of wearing corduroy

Topiary class

Classical sculpture appreciation class

Spotting yourself in the party pages of *Tatler* hour

Duck hunting

Billiards

Classical music appreciation afternoon

Dinner party discussion topic class (e.g. how the working classes smell)

However, the main reason why Joe hated going to St Cuthbert's wasn't the silly subjects. It was the fact that everyone at the school looked down on him. They thought that someone whose papa made their money from bog rolls was just too, too frightfully common.

"I want to go to a different school, Dad," said Joe.

"No problem. I can afford to send you to the poshest schools in the world. I heard about this place in Switzerland. You ski in the morning and then—"

"No," said Joe. "How about I go to the local comp?"

"*What*?" said Mr Spud.

"I might make a friend there," said Joe. He'd seen the kids milling around the school gates when he was being chauffeured to St Cuthbert's. They all looked like they were having such a great time – chatting, playing games, swapping cards. To Joe, it all looked so fabulously *normal*.

"Yes, but the local comp..." said Mr Spud, incredulously. "Are you *sure*?"

"Yes," replied Joe, defiantly.

"I could build you a school in the back garden if you like?" offered Mr Spud.

"No. I want to go to a normal school. With normal kids. I want to make a *friend*, Dad. I don't have a single friend at St Cuthbert's."

"But you can't go to a normal school. You are a billionaire, boy. All the kids will either bully you or want to be friends with you just because you are rich. It'll be a nightmare for you."

"Well, then I won't tell anyone who I am. I'll just be Joe. And maybe, just maybe, I'll make a friend, or even two…"

Mr Spud thought for a moment, and then relented. "If that's what you really want, Joe, then OK, you can go to a normal school."

Joe was so excited he bumjumped* along the sofa nearer to his dad to give him a cuddle.

"Don't crease the suit, boy," said Mr Spud.

[*Bumjumping (verb) *bum-jump-ing*. To move places while sitting using only your bottom to power you, thus meaning you do not have to get up. Much favoured by the overweight.]

"Sorry Dad," said Joe, bumjumping back a little. He cleared his throat. "Um... I love you, Dad."

"Yes, son, ditto, ditto," said Mr Spud, as he rose to his feet. "Well, have a good birthday, mate."

"Aren't we going to do something together tonight?" said Joe, trying to hide his disappointment. When he was younger, Joe's dad would always take him to the local burger restaurant as a birthday treat. They couldn't afford the burgers, so they would just order the chips, and eat them with some ham and pickle sandwiches that Mr Spud would smuggle in under his hat.

"I can't son, sorry. I've got a date with this beautiful girl tonight," said Mr Spud, indicating Page 3 of the *Sun*.

Joe looked at the page. There was a photograph of a woman whose clothes seemed to have fallen off. Her hair was dyed white blonde and she had so much make-up on it was difficult to tell if she was pretty or not. Underneath the image it read, 'Sapphire, 19, from Bradford. Likes shopping, hates thinking.'

"Don't you think Sapphire's a little young for you, Dad?" asked Joe.

"It's only a twenty-seven-year age gap," replied Mr Spud in an instant.

Joe wasn't convinced. "Well, where are you taking this Sapphire?"

"A nightclub."

"A *nightclub*?" asked Joe.

"Yes," said Mr Spud, in an offended tone. "I am not too old to go to a nightclub!" As he spoke he opened a box and pulled out what looked like a hamster that had been flattened by a mallet and put it on his head.

"What on earth is that, Dad?"

"What's what, Joe?" replied Mr Spud with mock innocence, as he adjusted the contraption to cover his bald dome.

"That thing on your head."

"Ooh, this. It's a toupee, boy! Only ten grand each. I bought a blonde one, a brown one, a ginger one, and an afro for special occasions. It makes me look twenty years younger, don't you think?"

Joe didn't like to lie. The toupee didn't make his dad look younger – instead, it made him look like a man who was trying to balance a dead rodent on his head. Therefore, Joe chose a non-committal, "Mmm."

"Right. Well, have a good night," Joe added, picking up the remote. It looked like it would be just him and the 100-inch TV again.

"There's some caviar in the fridge for your tea, son," said Mr Spud as he headed for the door.

"What's caviar?"

"It's fish eggs, son."

"Eurgh…" Joe didn't even like normal eggs much. Eggs laid by a fish sounded really revolting.

"Yeah, I had some on toast for me breakfast. It's absolutely disgusting, but it is very expensive so we should start eating it."

"Can't we just have bangers and mash or fish

and chips or Shepherd's Pie or something, Dad?"

"Mmm, I used to love Shepherd's Pie, son…" Mr Spud drooled a little, as if imagining the taste of Shepherd's Pie.

"Well then…?"

Mr Spud shook his head impatiently. "No no no, we are rich son! We have to eat all this posh stuff now like proper rich people do. See you later!" The door slammed behind him and moments later Joe heard the deafening roar of his father's lime-green Lamborghini speeding off into the night.

Joe was disappointed to be on his own again, but he still couldn't suppress a small smile as he turned on the TV. He was going to go to an ordinary school again and be an ordinary boy. And maybe, *just maybe*, make a friend.

The question was, how long could Joe keep the fact that he was a billionaire a secret…?

3

Who's the Fattiest?

Finally, the big day came. Joe took off his diamond-encrusted watch and put his gold pen in the drawer. He looked at the designer black snakeskin bag his dad had bought him for his first day at his new school and put it back in his cupboard. Even the bag that bag had *come in* was too posh, but he found an old plastic one in the kitchen and put his school books in that. Joe was determined not to stand out.

From the back seat of his chauffeur-driven Rolls Royce he had passed the local comprehensive many times on his way to St Cuthbert's, and seen the kids pouring out of the school. A rushing river of swinging bags and swear words and hair gel. Today, he was going to enter the gates for the first time. But he didn't want to arrive by Rolls Royce – that would be a pretty good hint to the other kids that he was rich. He instructed the chauffeur to drop him off at a nearby bus stop. It had been quite a few years since he had travelled by public transport, and as he waited at the bus stop Joe tingled with excitement.

"I can't change that!" said the bus driver.

Joe hadn't realised that a £50 note was not going to be welcome to pay for a two-pound fare, and had to get off the bus. Sighing, he began to walk the two miles to school, his flabby thighs rubbing together as he took each step.

Finally, Joe reached the school gates. For a moment he loitered nervously outside. He had spent so long living a life of wealth and privilege – how on earth was he going to fit in with these kids? Joe took a deep breath and marched across the playground.

At registration, there was only one other kid sitting on his own. Joe looked over at him. He was fat, just like Joe, with a mop of curly hair. When he saw Joe looking at him, he smiled. And when registration was finished, he came over.

"I'm Bob," said the fat boy.

"Hi Bob," replied Joe. The bell had just rung and they waddled along the corridor to the first lesson of the day. "I'm Joe," he added. It was weird to be in a school where no one knew who he was. Where he wasn't Bum Boy, or Billionaire Bum, or the Bumfresh Kid.

"I am so glad you're here, Joe. In the class I mean."

"Why's that?" asked Joe. He was excited. It

looked like he might have found his first friend already!

"Because I'm not the fattest boy in the school anymore," Bob said confidently, as if stating an independently verified fact.

Joe scowled, then stopped for a second and studied Bob. It looked to him like he and the other boy were about the same level of fattiness.

"How much do you weigh then?" demanded Joe grumpily.

"Well, how much do you weigh?" said Bob.

"Well, I asked you first."

Bob paused for a second. "About eight stone."

"I'm seven stone," said Joe, lying.

"No way are you seven stone!" said Bob angrily. "I'm twelve stone and you are much fatter than me!"

"You just said you were eight stone!" said Joe accusingly.

"I *was* eight stone…" replied Bob, "when I was a baby."

That afternoon it was cross-country running. What a dreadful ordeal for any day at school, not least your first day. It was a yearly torture that seemed designed solely to humiliate those kids who weren't sporty. A category Bob and Joe could definitely be squeezed into.

"Where is your running kit, Bob?" shouted Mr Bruise, the sadistic PE teacher, as Bob made his way onto the playing field. Bob was wearing his Y-fronts and vest, and his appearance was greeted by a huge wave of laughter from the other kids.

"S-s-s-someone m-m-must have hidden it S-s-s-sir," answered a shivering Bob.

"Likely story!" scoffed Mr Bruise. Like most PE teachers, it was difficult to imagine him

wearing anything other than a tracksuit.

"D-d-do I still have to do the r-r-r-r-run S-s-s-s-s-s-sir….?" asked a hopeful Bob.

"Oh yes, boy! You don't get off that easily. Right everyone, on your marks, get set… wait for it! GO!"

At first, Joe and Bob sprinted away like all the other kids, but after about three seconds they were both out of breath and were forced to walk. Soon everyone else had disappeared into the distance and the two fat boys were left alone.

"I come last every year," said Bob, unwrapping a Snickers and taking a large bite. "All the other kids always laugh at me. They get showered and dressed and wait at the finish line. They could all go home, but instead they wait just to jeer at me."

Joe frowned. That didn't sound like fun. He decided he didn't want to be last, and quickened his pace a little, making sure he was at least half a step ahead of Bob.

Bob glared at him, and piled on the speed, going up to at least half a mile an hour. From the determined expression on his face, Joe knew that

Bob was hoping that this year was his golden chance not to finish last.

Joe sped up a little more. They were now almost jogging. The race was on. For the ultimate prize: who was going to finish... second to last! Joe really didn't want to be beaten at cross-country running by a fat boy in his vest and pants on his first day at school.

After what seemed like an eternity the finish line hazed into sight. Both boys were out of breath with all this power-waddling.

Suddenly, disaster struck Joe. A painful stitch burst in his side.

"Ooww!" cried Joe.

"What's the matter?" asked Bob, now quite a few centimetres in the lead.

"I've got a stitch... I've got to stop. Owww..."

"You're bluffing. A fifteen-stone girl pulled

that on me last year and ended up beating me by a fraction of a second."

"Oww. It's true," said Joe, holding his side tightly.

"I ain't falling for it, Joe. You are going to be last, and this year all the kids in the year are gonna be laughing at you!" said Bob triumphantly, as he edged ahead still further.

Being laughed at on his first day at school was the last thing Joe wanted. He'd had enough of being laughed at when he was at St Cuthbert's. However, the stitch was becoming more and more painful with every step. It was as if it was burning a hole in his side. "How about I give you a fiver to come last?" he said.

"No way," replied Bob, through heaving breaths.

"A tenner?"

"No."

"Twenty quid?"

"Try harder."

"Fifty quid."

Bob stopped, and looked around at Joe.

"Fifty quid…" he said. "That's a lot of chocolate."

"Yeah," said Joe. "Tons."

"You've got yourself a deal. But I want the wonga now."

Joe searched through his shorts and pulled out a fifty-pound note.

"What's that?" asked Bob.

"It's a fifty pound note."

"I've never seen one before. Where did you get it?"

"Oh, erm, it was my birthday last week you see…" said Joe, stumbling over his words a little. "And my dad gave me that as a present."

The marginally fatter boy studied it for a moment, holding it up to the light as if it was a priceless artefact. "Wow. Your dad must be *loaded*," he said.

The truth would have blown Bob's fat mind. That Mr Spud had given his son two million pounds as a birthday present. So Joe kept schtum.

"Nah, not really," he said.

"Go on then," said Bob. "I'll come last again. For fifty quid I would finish tomorrow if you like."

"Just a few paces behind me will be fine," said Joe. "Then it will look real."

Joe edged ahead, still gripping his side in pain. Hundreds of little cruelly smiling faces were coming into focus now. The new boy crossed the finish line with only a hum of mocking laughter. Trailing behind was Bob, clutching his fifty-pound note, since there were no pockets in his Y-fronts. As he neared the finish line the kids started chanting.

"BLOB! BLOB! BLOB! BLOB!
BLOB! BLOB! BLOB! BLOB!
BLOB! BLOB! BLOB! BLOB!
BLOB! BLOB! BLOB! BLOB!
BLOB! BLOB! BLOB!"

The chants grew louder and louder.

"BLOB! BLOB! BLOB!
BLOB! BLOB! BLOB!
BLOB! BLOB! BLOB!
BLOB! BLOB! BLOB!
BLOB! BLOB! BLOB!
BLOB! BLOB! BLOB!
BLOB! BLOB! BLOB!
BLOB! BLOB! BLOB!
BLOB! BLOB! BLOB!
BLOB! BLOB! BLOB!
BLOB! BLOB! BLOB!
BLOB! BLOB! BLOB!"

They started clapping in time now.

BLOB! BLOB! BLOB! BLOB!
BLOB! BLOB! BLOB! BLOB!
BLOB! BLOB! BLOB! BLOB!
BLOB! BLOB! BLOB! BLOB!
BLOB! BLOB! BLOB! BLOB!
BLOB! BLOB! BLOB! BLOB!
BLOB! BLOB! BLOB! BLOB!
BLOB! BLOB! BLOB! BLOB!
BLOB! BLOB! BLOB! BLOB!
BLOB! BLOB! BLOB! BLOB!
BLOB! BLOB! BLOB! BLOB!
BLOB! BLOB! BLOB! BLOB!
BLOB! BLOB! BLOB! BLOB!
BLOB! BLOB! BLOB! BLOB!
BLOB! BLOB!"

Undeterred, Bob hurled his body across the finish line.

"HA! HA! HA! HA!
HA! HA! HA! HA! HA!
HA! HA! HA! HA! HA!
HA! HA! HA! HA! HA! HA! HA!
HA! HA! HA! HA! HA! HA! HA!
HA! HA! HA! HA! HA! HA!
HA! HA! HA! HA! HA!
HA! HA! HA! HA! HA!
HA! HA! HA! HA! HA!

HA! HA! HA! HA! HA!
HA! HA! HA! HA! HA!
HA! HA! HA! HA! HA! HA!
HA! HA! HA! HA! HA! HA! HA!
HA! HA! HA! HA! HA! HA! HA!
HA! HA! HA! HA! HA! HA! HA!
HA!"

The other kids fell around laughing, pointing
at Bob, as he bent over and panted for breath.

Turning around, Joe felt a sudden twinge of guilt. As the school kids dispersed, he went over to Bob and helped him stand up straight.

"Thanks," said Joe.

"You're welcome," said Bob. "To be honest I should have done that anyway. If you came last on your very first day, you'd never hear the end of it. But next year you're on your own. I don't care if you give me a million pounds – I ain't coming last again!"

Joe thought about his two million pound birthday cheque. "What about two million pounds?" he joked.

"Deal!" said Bob, laughing. "Imagine if you really did have that much money. It would be crazy! I guess you could have everything you ever wanted!"

Joe forced a smile. "Yeah," he said. "Maybe..."

4

"Loo Rolls?"

"So, did you forget your kit on purpose?" asked Joe.

Mr Bruise had locked up the changing rooms by the time Joe and Bob had finished their cross-country run… well, cross-country walk. They stood outside the grey concrete building, Bob shivering in his pants. They'd already been to find the school secretary, but there was absolutely no one left in the whole place. Well, apart from the caretaker. Who didn't seem to speak English. Or any other language for that matter.

"No," replied Bob, a little hurt at the suggestion. "I may not be the fastest runner, but I'm not that much of a coward."

They trudged through the school grounds, Joe in his singlet and shorts, and Bob in his vest and pants. They looked like two rejects from a boy band audition.

"So who took it?" said Joe.

"I dunno. It might be the Grubbs. They're the school bullies."

"The Grubbs?"

"Yeah. They're twins."

"Oh," said Joe. "I haven't met them yet."

"You will," replied Bob, dolefully. "You know, I feel really bad about taking your birthday money off you…"

"You don't have to," said Joe. "It's fine."

"But fifty pounds is a lot of money," Bob protested.

Fifty pounds was not a lot of money to the Spuds. Here are a few things Joe and his dad would do with fifty-pound notes:

- Light them instead of bits of old newspaper to get the barbecue going
- Keep a pad of them by the telephone and use them as post-it notes
- Line the hamster cage with handfuls of them and then throw them out after a week when they began to smell of hamster wee

- Let the same hamster use one as a towel after it's had a shower
- Filter coffee through them
- Make paper hats out of them to wear on Christmas day
- Blow their noses on them
- Spit chewed-up chewing gum into them before crumpling them and placing them in the hand of a butler who would then put them in the hand of a footman who would then put them in the hand of a maid who would then put them in the bin
- Make paper aeroplanes out of them and throw them at each other
- Wallpaper the downstairs loo with them

"I never asked," said Bob. "What does your dad do?"

Joe panicked for a moment. "Erm, he, er, he makes loo rolls," he said, only lying a tiny bit.

"*Loo rolls?*" said Bob. He couldn't suppress his smile.

"Yes," replied Joe defiantly. "He makes loo rolls."

Bob stopped smiling. "That doesn't sound like it pays all that well."

Joe winced. "Er… no, it doesn't."

"Then I guess your dad had to save for weeks to give you £50. Here you go." Bob carefully handed the now-slightly-crumpled fifty-pound note back to Joe.

"No, you keep it," protested Joe.

Bob pressed the note into Joe's hand. "It's your birthday money. You keep it."

Joe smiled uncertainly and closed his hand

over the money. "Thank you, Bob. So, what does *your* dad do?"

"My dad died last year."

They continued walking in silence for a moment. All Joe could hear was the sound of his heart beating. He couldn't think of anything to say. All he knew was that he felt awful for his new friend. Then he remembered that when someone died people sometimes said, 'I'm sorry'.

"I'm sorry," he said.

"It's not your fault," said Bob.

"I mean, well, I'm sorry he died."

"I'm sorry too."

"How did he… you know?"

"Cancer. It was really scary. He just got more and more ill and then one day they took me out of school and I went to the hospital. We sat by his bed for ages and you could hear his breath rattling and then suddenly the sound just stopped. I ran outside to get the nurse and she came in and said he was 'gone'. It's just me and my mum now."

"What does your mum do?"

"She works at Tesco. On the checkout. That's where she met my dad. He would shop on Saturday mornings. He used to joke that he 'only came in for a pint of milk but left with a wife!'"

"It sounds like he was funny," said Joe.

"He was," said Bob, smiling. "Mum's got another job too. She's a cleaner at an old people's home in the evenings. Just to make ends meet."

"Wow," said Joe. "Doesn't she get tired?"

"Yeah," said Bob. "So I do a lot of the cleaning and stuff."

Joe felt really sorry for Bob. Since he was eight, Joe had never had to do anything at home – there was always the butler or the maid or gardener or the chauffeur or whoever to do everything. He took the note out of his pocket. If there was one person who needed the money more than him it was Bob. "Please, Bob, keep the £50."

"No. I don't want to. I'd feel bad."

"Well, let me at least buy you some chocolate."

"You've got a deal," said Bob. "Let's go to Raj's."

5

Out of Date Easter Eggs

DING!

No, reader, that's not your doorbell. No need to get up. It's the sound of the bell tinkling in Raj's shop as Bob and Joe opened the door.

"Ah, Bob! My favourite customer!" said Raj. "Welcome, welcome!"

Raj ran the local newsagent's shop. All the local kids adored him. He was like the funny uncle you always wished you had. And even better than that, he sold sweets.

"Hi, Raj!" said Bob. 'This is Joe."

"Hello Joe," exclaimed Raj. "Two fat boys in

my shop at one time! The Lord must be smiling on me today! Why have you both got so little on?"

"We came straight from cross-country running Raj," explained Bob.

"Fantastic! How did you do?"

"First and second…" replied Bob.

"That's wonderful!" exclaimed Raj.

"…to last," finished Bob.

"That's not so good. But I imagine you boys must be hungry after all that exercise. How can I help you today?"

"We'd like to buy some chocolate," said Joe.

"Well, you have come to the right place. I have the finest selection of chocolate bars in this parade!" Raj announced triumphantly. Considering the only other shops in the parade were a launderette and a long since closed florist that wasn't saying much, but the boys let it pass.

Now, one thing Joe knew for certain was that chocolate didn't have to be expensive to taste nice. In fact, after a few years of gorging themselves on the finest chocolates from Belgium or Switzerland, he and his dad had realised that they weren't half as delicious as a Yorkie. Or a bag of Minstrels.

Or, for the true connoisseur, a Double Decker.

"Well, let me know if I can help you gentlemen," said the newsagent. The stock in Raj's shop was haphazardly laid out. Why was *Nuts* magazine next to the Tipp-ex? If you couldn't find the Jelly Tots, it was entirely possible that they might be hiding under a copy of the *Sun* from 1982. And did the post-it notes really have to be in the freezer?

However, local people kept coming to the shop because they loved Raj, and he loved his customers too, particularly Bob. Bob was one of his absolute best customers.

"We are happy just to browse thanks," replied Bob. He was studying the rows and rows of confectionery, looking for something special. And today money wasn't a problem. Joe had a fifty-pound note in his pocket. They could even afford one of Raj's out of date Easter eggs.

"The Wispas are very good today, young Sirs. Fresh in this morning," ventured Raj.

"We are just looking thank you," replied Bob politely.

"The Cadbury's Creme Eggs are in season," suggested the newsagent.

"Thank you," said Joe politely, smiling.

"Just to say, gentlemen, I am here to help," said Raj. "If you have any questions please don't hesitate to ask."

"We will," said Joe.

There was a brief moment of silence.

"Just to let you know the Flake is off today, Sirs," continued Raj. "I should have said. A problem with the supplier, but I should have them back on sale tomorrow."

"Thanks for letting us know," said Bob. He and Joe shared a look. They were beginning to wish the newsagent would let them shop in peace.

"I can recommend a Ripple. I had one earlier and they are exquisite at the moment."

Joe nodded politely.

"I'll leave you alone to make up your own mind. As I say, I am here to help."

"Can I have one of these?" said Bob, lifting up a giant bar of Cadbury's Dairy Milk to show Joe.

Joe laughed. "Of course you can!"

"An excellent choice, gentlemen. I have those on special offer today. Buy ten get one free," said Raj.

"I think we just need the one right now, Raj," said Bob.

"Buy five get half a one free?"

"No thanks," said Joe. "How much is it?"

"£3.20 please."

Joe took out the fifty-pound note.

Raj looked at it in wonder. "Oh my! I have never seen one of those before. You must be a very rich young man!"

"Not at all," said Joe.

"His dad gave it to him for his birthday," chimed in Bob.

"Lucky boy," said Raj. He peered at Joe. "You know, you look familiar, young man."

"Do I?" replied Joe nervously.

"Yes I am sure I have seen you somewhere before." Raj tapped his chin as he thought. Bob stared at him, baffled. "Yes," said Raj eventually. "Only the other day I saw a picture of you in a magazine."

"I doubt it, Raj," scoffed Bob. "His dad

makes loo rolls!"

"That's it!" exclaimed Raj. He riffled through a pile of old newspapers and pulled out the *Sunday Times Rich List*.

Joe started to panic. "I've got to go…"

The newsagent flicked through the pages. "There you are!" Raj indicated a photograph of Joe sitting awkwardly on the front of his Formula One racing car, and then read aloud from the magazine. "Britain's Richest Children. Number one: Joe Spud, age twelve. Bumfresh heir. Estimated worth, ten billion."

A large lump of chocolate dropped from Bob's mouth onto the floor. "Ten *billion*?"

"No way have I got ten billion," protested Joe. "The press always exaggerate. I've got eight billion at the most. And I won't even get most of it till I'm older."

"That's still a lot of money!" exclaimed Bob.

"Yes, I suppose it is."

"Why didn't you tell me? I thought we were mates."

"I'm sorry," stammered Joe. "I just wanted to be normal. And it's so embarrassing being the son of a bog-roll billionaire."

"No no no you should be proud of your dad!" exclaimed Raj. "His story is an inspiration to all of us. A humble man who became a billionaire with one simple idea!"

Joe had never really thought of his dad like that.

"Leonard Spud revolutionised the way we wipe our bottoms forever!" Raj chuckled.

"Thanks, Raj."

"Now, please tell your father I have just started using Bumfresh and I love it! My bottom has never been so sparkling! See you next time!"

The two boys walked along the street in

silence. All you could hear was Bob sucking the chocolate from between his teeth.

"You lied to me," said Bob.

"Well I did tell you he worked in bog rolls," said Joe, uncomfortably.

"Yeah but…"

"I know. I'm sorry." It was Joe's first day at school, and his secret was already out. "Here, have the change," said Joe, reaching in his pocket for the two twenty-pound notes.

Bob looked crushed. "I don't want your money."

"But I'm a billionaire," said Joe. "And my dad's got squillions. I don't even know what that means, but I know it's loads. Just take it. Here, have this lot too." He pulled out a roll of £50 notes.

"I don't want it," said Bob.

Joe's face crinkled with incredulity. "Why not?"

"Because I don't care about your money. I just liked hanging out with you today."

Joe smiled. "And I liked hanging out with you." He coughed. "Look, I really am sorry. It's just… the kids at my old school used to bully me because I was the Bumfresh boy. I wanted to just be a normal kid."

"I can understand that," said Bob. "I mean, it would be nice to start again."

"Yeah," said Joe.

Bob stopped, and held out his hand. "I'm Bob," he said.

Joe shook his hand. "Joe Spud."

"No other secrets?"

"No," said Joe, smiling. "That's it."

"Good," said Bob, smiling too.

"You won't tell anyone at school, will you?" said Joe. "About me being a billionaire. It's so embarrassing. Especially when they find out how my dad became rich. Please?"

"Not if you don't want me to."

"I don't. I really don't."

"Well, I won't then."

"Thanks."

The two continued down the street. After a few paces Joe couldn't wait any longer. He turned to Bob, who had already polished off half the massive bar of Dairy Milk. "Can I have some chocolate then?" he asked.

"Yes of course. This is for us to share," said Bob, as he broke off his friend a tiny square of chocolate.

6

The Grubbs

"OI! BLOB!" came a shout from behind them.

"Just keep walking," said Bob.

Joe turned to look around and glimpsed a pair of twins. They looked terrifying – like gorillas in human suits. These must be the dreaded Grubbs Bob had talked about.

"Don't look round," said Bob. "I'm serious. Just keep walking."

Joe was beginning to wish he was luxuriating in the safety of the back seat of his chauffeur-driven Rolls Royce, rather than walking to the bus stop.

"FATSO!"

As Joe and Bob walked faster, they could hear footsteps behind them. Although it was still early, the winter sky was blackening. The street lamps flickered on and blotches of yellow light spilled onto the wet ground.

"Quick, let's run down here," said Bob. The boys dashed down an alley, and hid behind a giant green wheely bin that was parked at the back of a Bella Pasta.

"I think we've lost them," whispered Bob.

"Are those the Grubbs?" asked Joe.

"Shh. Keep your voice down!"

"Sorry," whispered Joe.

"Yeah, it's the Grubbs."

"The ones who bully you?"

"That's them. They're identical twins. Dave and Sue Grubb."

"*Sue*? One of them's a girl?" Joe could swear that when he'd turned around and seen the twins following them, both of them had thick facial hair.

"Sue's a girl, yes," said Bob, as if Joe was some kind of idiot.

"Then they can't be identical," whispered Joe. "I mean, if one's a boy and one's a girl."

"Well, yes, but no one can tell them apart."

Suddenly Joe and Bob heard footsteps coming closer and closer.

"I can smell fat boys!" came a voice from the other side of the bin. The Grubbs wheeled the bin away to reveal the two boys crouching behind it. Joe took his first good look at the pair. Bob was right. The Grubbs were identical. They both had matching crew-cuts, hairy knuckles and moustaches. All of which seemed unfortunate for both of them.

Let's play spot the difference with the Grubbs.

Can you spot the ten differences between these two?

No you can't. They are exactly the same.

A gust of cold wind hummed through the alley. An empty can trundled past on the ground. Something twitched in the bushes.

"How was the cross-country run without your kit today Blob?" chuckled one Grubb.

"I knew that was you two!" Bob replied angrily. "So what did you do with it?"

"It's in the canal!" chuckled the other.

"Now give us your chocolate." Even hearing their voices didn't give any clues as to who was Dave and who was Sue. Both their voices wavered high and low in one sentence.

"I'm taking some home for my mum," protested Bob.

"I don't care," said the other Grubb.

"Give us it you little ****," said the other one.

I have to confess, reader, that the **** bit was a swear word. Other swear words include ****,

******** and of course the incredibly rude
*************************. If you don't know
any swear words it's best to ask a parent or
teacher or other responsible adult to make a list
for you.

For example, here are some of the rude words
I know:

Puttock

Krunter

Noog

Smagger

Mingmong

Klazbo

Furp

Fedger

Nadgers

Blimblam

Coobdrizz

Trunt

Joofer

Klootzak

Bullmunter

Gunder

Whizzplop

Huppeltrut

Bwatter

Lopcrock

Moozer

Frink

Dangle Spangles

Boola Boola

Burmnop

Oodplops

Lingpoop

Twutter

Ploomfizz

Lumweed

Moomers

Blamfan

Pognots

Voogan Bits

Zucky zuck

Sming

Kumbo Drops

Poot Puddle

Kungo

Bimbim

Paffer

Goollyging

Nonkey

Humbum

Ponk

Hool

Blunkers

Pumpum

Minki

Gruntbunt

Poob

Drazz

Nockynooters

Luzzer

Plimplam

Vart

All of those words are so rude I wouldn't dream of putting them in this book.

"Don't pick on him!" said Joe. Then he instantly regretted drawing attention to himself again as the Grubbs took a step towards him.

"Or what?" said either Dave or Sue, their breath toxic from a bag of Skips they had recently snatched from a little girl in year five.

"Or…" Joe searched his mind for something to say that would crush these bullies forever. "Or I'll be very disappointed with you both."

That wasn't it.

The Grubbs laughed. They snatched what was left of the Cadbury's Dairy Milk bar from Bob's hand and then grabbed his arms. They lifted him up and, as Bob yelled for help, they deposited him into the wheely bin. Before Joe could say anything else the Grubbs were stomping off down the road laughing, with their mouths full of stolen chocolate.

Joe dragged a wooden crate over, then stood on it to give himself more height. He leaned down into the bin and caught hold of Bob under the armpits. With a great heave, he started to pull his heavy friend out of the bin.

"Are you OK?" he asked, as he strained to take Bob's weight.

"Oh, yeah. They do this to me most days," said Bob. He pulled some spaghetti and parmesan cheese out of his curly hair – some of it might have been there since the last time the Grubb twins deposited him in a bin.

"Well, why don't you tell your mum?"

"I don't want to make her worry about me. She's got enough to worry about already," replied Bob.

"Maybe you should tell a teacher then."

"The Grubbs said if I ever told anyone that they would really beat me up. They know where I live and even if they got expelled they could still find me," said Bob. He looked like he was about to cry. Joe didn't like to see his new friend upset. "One day, I'll get them back. I will. My dad always used to say the best way to beat bullies is to stand up to them. One day I will."

Joe looked at his new friend. Standing there in his underwear, covered in scraps of Italian food. He thought of Bob standing up to the Grubbs. The fat boy would get massacred.

But maybe there's another way, he thought. *Maybe I can get the Grubbs off his back forever.*

He smiled. He still felt bad about paying Bob to come last in the race. Now he could make up for it. If his plan worked, he and Bob were going to be more than just friends. They'd be *best* friends.

7

Gerbils on Toast

"I bought you something," said Joe. He and Bob were sitting on the bench in the playground, watching the more agile kids play football.

"Just because you are a billionaire, doesn't mean you have to buy me anything," said Bob.

"I know, but..." Joe brought a large bar of Dairy Milk out of his bag. Bob's eyes couldn't help but light up a little.

"We can share it," said Joe, before snapping off a tiny square of chocolate. Then breaking that tiny square in half.

Bob's face fell.

"I'm only joking!" said Joe. "Here." He handed Bob the bar to help himself.

"Oh, no," said Bob.

"What?" said Joe.

Bob pointed. The Grubbs were walking slowly across the playground towards them, right through the games of football. Not that anyone dared to complain.

"Quick, let's make a run for it," said Bob.

"Where?"

"The dining room. They wouldn't dare go in there. No one does."

"Why?"

"You'll see."

When they burst into the dining room it was completely empty, aside from a lone dinner lady.

The Grubbs burst in a few paces behind them,

their genders still uncertain.

"If you aren't eating, get out!' shouted Mrs Trafe.

"But Mrs Trafe...?" said either Dave or Sue.

"I SAID 'OUT'!"

The twins reluctantly retreated, as Joe and Bob tentatively made their way to the serving counter.

Mrs Trafe was a large, smiley soul, of dinner-lady age. Bob had explained on the way to the canteen that she was nice enough, but her food was truly revolting. The kids in the school would rather die than eat anything she cooked. In fact they probably *would* die if they ate anything she cooked.

"Who's that, then?" said Mrs Trafe, peering at Joe.

"This is my friend, Joe," said Bob.

Despite the vile smell in the canteen, Joe felt

warmth spread through him. No one had ever called him their friend before!

"Now what would you like today, boys?" Mrs Trafe said with a warm smile. "I have a very nice badger and onion pie. Some deep-fried rust. Or for the vegetarians I have jacket potatoes with sock cheese."

"Mmm, it all looks so nice," said Bob, lying, as the Grubbs stared in at them through the grimy windows.

Mrs Trafe's cooking was truly unspeakable. A typical week's menu for the school canteen looked like this:

Monday

Soup of the day – wasp

Gerbils on toast

Or

Hair lasagne (vegetarian option)

Or

Brick cutlet

All served with deep-fried cardboard

Dessert – A slice of sweat cake

Tuesday

Soup of the day – Caterpillar consommé

Macaroni snot (vegetarian option)

Or

Road-kill bake

Or

Slipper frittata

All served with spider's web salad

Dessert – Toenail ice cream

Wednesday

Soup of the day – Cream of hedgehog

Parrot kedgeree (may contain nuts)

Or

Dandruff risotto

Or

Bread sandwich (slice of bread between
two slices of bread)

Or

Char-grilled kitten (healthy option)

Or

Soil bolognese

*All served with either boiled wood or
deep fried iron filings*

Dessert – Squirrel dropping tart with
cream or ice cream

Thursday: Indian Day

Soup of the Day – Turban

To start – Paper poppadoms (A4 or A3 sizes) with chutney

Main course – Wet-wipe tandoori (vegan)

Or

Moth korma (spicy)

Or

Newt vindaloo (very spicy)

All served with bogey bhajis

Dessert – a refreshing sand sorbet

Friday

Soup of the day – Terrapin

Pan-fried otter steaks

Or

Owl quiche (kosher)

Or

Boiled poodle (not suitable for

vegetarians)

All served with a slice of gravy

Dessert – Mouse mousse

"It's so hard to choose…" said Bob, desperately scouring the trays of food for something edible. "Mmm, I think we will just have two jacket potatoes please."

"Is there any chance I could have it without the sock cheese?" pleaded Joe.

Bob looked hopefully at Mrs Trafe.

"I could sprinkle on some ear-wax shavings if you prefer? Or a showering of dandruff?" offered Mrs Trafe with a smile.

"Mmm, I think I will just have it totally plain please," said Joe.

"Some boiled mould on the side perhaps? You are growing boys…" offered Mrs Trafe, wielding a serving spoon of something green and unspeakable.

"I'm on a diet, Mrs Trafe," said Joe.

"Me too," said Bob.

"That's a shame, boys," said the dinner lady

dolefully. "I have a smashing dessert on today. Jellyfish and custard."

"My absolute favourite too!" said Joe. "Never mind."

He took his tray to one of the empty tables and sat down. As he put his knife and fork into the potato he realised that Mrs Trafe had forgotten to cook it.

"How are your spuds?" called Mrs Trafe across the hall.

"Delicious, thank you, Mrs Trafe," Joe called back, as he pushed his raw potato round the plate. It was still covered in soil and he noticed a maggot burrowing out of it. "I hate it when they are too well done. This is perfect!"

"Good good!" she said.

Bob was trying to chew his but it was so utterly inedible he started crying.

"Something the matter, boy?" called Mrs Trafe.

"Oh no, it's so delicious that these are tears of joy!" said Bob.

DDDDDDDDDRrrrrrrrrriiiiiiiiiiiiNNNNNNNNNGGGGGGGGGGG!

Once again, that wasn't your doorbell, reader. That was the bell to signal the end of lunch.

Joe let out a sigh of relief. Dinner hour was over.

"Oh, what a shame, Mrs Trafe," said Joe. "We have to go to our Maths lesson now."

Mrs Trafe limped over and inspected their plates.

"You've hardly touched them!" she said.

"Sorry. It was just so filling. And really really tasty though," said Joe.

"Mmm," seconded Bob, still crying.

"Well it doesn't matter. I can put them in the

fridge for you and you can finish them off tomorrow."

Joe and Bob shared a horrified look.

"Really, I don't want you to go to any trouble," said Joe.

"No trouble at all. See you then. And I've got some specials tomorrow. It's the anniversary of the bombing of Pearl Harbour, so it's Japanese day. I'm doing my armpit hair sushi, followed by tadpole tempura... Boys...? Boys...?"

"I think the Grubbs have gone," said Bob as they sneaked out of the canteen. "I've just got to use the bog."

"I'll wait for you," said Joe. He leaned against the wall, as Bob disappeared through a door. Usually Joe would have said that the lavatories were smelly – and he'd have been horrified to have to use them, after the privacy of his own en-en-suite bathroom, with emperor-size bath.

But the truth was that the toilets didn't smell as bad as the canteen.

Suddenly Joe sensed two figures looming behind him. He didn't need to turn round. He knew it was the Grubbs.

"Where is he?" said one.

"He's in the boys' loo, but you can't go in there," said Joe. "Well, not both of you, anyway."

"Where's the chocolate bar?" asked the other.

"Bob's got it," said Joe.

"Well, we'll wait for him then," said the Grubb.

The other Grubb turned to Joe, a deadly look in its eye. "Now give us a pound. Unless you want a dead arm, that is."

Joe gulped. "Actually... I'm glad I bumped into you two guys, well, guy and a girl, obviously."

"Obviously," said Dave or Sue. "Give us a pound."

"Wait," said Joe. "It's just... I wondered if—"

"Give him a dead arm, Sue," said a Grubb, revealing for perhaps the first time which of the twins was male and which was female. But then the Grubbs grabbed Joe and spun him around, and he lost track again.

"No! Wait," said Joe. "The thing is, I want to make you two an offer..."

8

The Witch

DDDDDDDRRRRRRRIIIIIIIIINNN NNNNGGGGGGGGG!

"The bell is a signal for me, not you!" said Miss Spite sharply. Teachers love saying that. It's one of their catchphrases, as I'm sure you know. The all-time top ten of teachers' catchphrases goes like this:

At ten… "Walk, don't run!"

A non-mover at nine… "Are you chewing?"

Up three places to eight... "I can still hear talking."

A former number one at seven... "It doesn't need discussion."

A new entry at six... "How many times do you need to be told?"

Down one place at five... "Spelling!"

Another non-mover at four... "I will not tolerate litter!"

New at three... "Do you want to pass your GCSEs?"

Just missing the top spot at two... "Would you do that at home?"

And still at number one... "It's not just yourself you've let down, but the whole school."

Taking the History lesson was Miss Spite. Miss Spite smelt of rotten cabbage. That was the nicest thing about her. She was one of the school's most feared teachers. When she smiled she looked like a crocodile that was about to eat you. Miss Spite loved nothing more than giving out punishments, once suspending a girl for dropping a pea on the floor of the school canteen. "That pea could have had someone's eye out!" she had yelled.

Kids at the school had fun thinking up

nicknames for their teachers. Some were fond, others cruel. Mr Paxton the French teacher was 'Tomato', as he had a big round red face like a tomato. The headmaster, Mr Dust, was called 'The Tortoise' as he looked like one. He was very old, extremely wrinkly, and walked impossibly slowly. The deputy head, Mr Underhill, was 'Mr Underarms', as he ponged a bit, especially in the summer. And Mrs MacDonald, the biology teacher, was called either 'The Bearded Lady' or even 'Hairy Maclary from Donaldson's Dairy' as she… well, I imagine you can guess why.

But the kids just called Miss Spite 'The Witch'. It was the only name that really ever fitted and was passed down through generations of pupils at the school.

All the kids she taught passed their exams though. They were too scared not to.

"We still have the small matter of last night's

homework," Miss Spite announced with an evil relish that suggested she was desperate for someone to have failed to do it.

Joe reached his hand into his bag. Disaster. His exercise book wasn't there. He had spent all night writing this intensely boring 500-word essay about some old dead Queen, but in the rush to get to school on time he must have left it on his bed.

Oh, no, he thought. *Oh no no no no no...*

Joe looked over at Bob, but all his friend could do was grimace sympathetically.

Miss Spite stalked the classroom like a Tyrannosaurus Rex deciding which little creature it was going to eat first. To her evident disappointment, a field of grubby little hands held aloft essay after essay. She gathered them up, before stopping at Spud.

"Miss...?" he stammered.

"Yeeeessss Ssspppuuudddd?" said Miss Spite, drawing out her words as long as possible so she could relish this delicious moment.

"I did do it, but..."

"Oh yes, of course you did it!" The Witch cackled. All the other pupils except Bob sniggered too. There was nothing more pleasurable than seeing someone else get into trouble.

"I left it at home."

"Litter duty!" the teacher snapped.

"I am not lying, Miss. And my dad will be at home today, I could—"

"I should have known. Your father is clearly penniless and on the dole, sitting at home watching daytime TV – much as you will no doubt be doing in ten years' time. Yes...?"

Joe and Bob couldn't help but share a smirk at this.

"Er..." said Joe. "If I called him and asked

him to run the essay over here would you believe me?"

Miss Spite smiled broadly. She was going to enjoy this.

"Spud, I will give you fifteen minutes exactly to place said essay in my hand. I hope your father is quick."

"But—" started Joe.

"No 'buts' boy. Fifteen minutes."

"Well thank you Miss," said Joe sarcastically.

"You're quite welcome," said the Witch. "I like to think that everyone gets a fair chance to rectify their errors in my class."

She turned to the rest of the class. "The rest of you are dismissed," she said.

Kids started to spill out into the corridor. Miss Spite leaned after them and screamed, "Walk, don't run!"

Miss Spite couldn't resist another catchphrase.

She was the queen of the catchphrase. And now she couldn't stop.

"It doesn't need discussion!" she called after her pupils, randomly. Miss Spite was on a roll now. "Are you chewing?" she howled down the corridor to a passing school inspector.

"Fifteen minutes, Miss?" said Joe.

Miss Spite studied her little antique watch. "Fourteen minutes, fifty one seconds, in point of fact."

Joe gulped. Was Dad going to be able to get there that fast?

9

"Finger?"

"Finger?" asked Bob, as he offered half of his Twix to his friend.

"Thank you, mate," said Joe. They stood in a quiet corner of the playground and contemplated Joe's bleak fate.

"What are you going to do?"

"I dunno. I texted my dad. But there's no way he can get here in fifteen minutes. What can I do?"

A few ideas raced through Joe's mind.

He could invent a time machine and travel

back in time and remember not to forget his homework. It might be a bit hard to do though, as if time machines *had* ever been invented then maybe someone would have come back from the future and prevented Piers Morgan's birth.

Joe could go back to the classroom and tell Miss Spite that 'the tiger had eaten it'. This would only be half a lie, as they did have a private zoo and a tiger. Called Geoff. And an alligator called Jenny.

Become a nun. He would have to live in a nunnery and spend his days saying prayers and singing hymns and doing general religious stuff. On the one hand the nunnery would give him sanctuary from Miss Spite and he did look good in black, but on the other hand it might get a bit boring.

Go and live on another planet. Venus is nearest, but it might be safer to go to Neptune.

Live the rest of his life underground. Perhaps even start a tribe of below-the-surface-of-the-earth dwellers and create a whole secret society of people who all owed Miss Spite some homework.

Have plastic surgery and change his identity. Then live the rest of his life as an old lady called Winnie.

Become invisible. Joe wasn't sure how this might be achieved.

Run to the local bookshop and buy a copy of *How to Learn Mind Control in Ten Minutes* by Professor Stephen Haste and very quickly hypnotise Miss Spite into thinking he had already given her his homework.

Disguise himself as a plate of spaghetti Bolognese.

Bribe the school nurse into telling Miss Spite he had died.

Hide in a bush for the rest of his life. He could survive on a diet of worms and grubs.

Paint himself blue and claim to be a Smurf.

Joe had barely had time to consider these options when two familiar shadows loomed behind them.

"Bob," said one of them, in a voice neither high nor low enough to determine its gender.

The boys turned around. Bob, tired of

fighting, simply handed them his slightly nibbled finger of Twix.

"Don't worry," he whispered to Joe. "I've concealed a large number of Smarties down my sock."

"We don't want your Twix," said Grubb number one.

"No?" said Bob. His mind started racing. Could the Grubbs possibly know about the Smarties?

"No, we wanted to say we are very sorry for bullying you," said Grubb number two.

"And as a peace gesture we would like to invite you round for tea," prompted Grubb number one.

'Tea?" asked Bob, incredulous.

"Yes, and maybe we can all play Hungry Hippos together," continued Grubb number two.

Bob looked at his friend, but Joe just shrugged.

"Thank you, guys, I mean guy and girl, obviously…"

"Obviously," said an unidentified Grubb.

"…but I am a bit busy tonight," continued Bob.

"Maybe another time," said a Grubb, as the twins lolloped off.

"That was weird," said Bob, retrieving some Smarties that now had a faint taste of sock. "I couldn't imagine a night when I would want to go and play Hungry Hippos with those two. Even if I lived until I was a hundred."

"Yeah, how strange…" said Joe. He glanced away quickly.

At that moment, a deafening roar silenced the playground. Joe looked up. A helicopter was hovering overhead. Very quickly all the football games broke up, and the kids raced out of the way of the descending aircraft. Items from hundreds of packed lunches were whisked up in the air by the force of the blades. Packets of Quavers, a mint-chocolate Aero, even a Müller Fruit Corner danced about in the whirling air, before smashing to the ground as the engine shut down and the blades slowed to a stop.

Mr Spud leaped out of the passenger seat and raced across the playground holding the essay.

Oh no! thought Joe.

Mr Spud was wearing a brown toupee that he held on to his head with both hands, and an all-in-one gold jumpsuit with 'BUM AIR'

emblazoned on the back in sparkly letters. Joe felt like he was going to die of embarrassment. He tried to hide himself behind one of the older kids. However, he was too fat and his dad spotted him.

"Joe! Joe! There you are!" shouted Mr Spud.

All the other kids stared at Joe Spud. They hadn't paid much attention to this short fat new boy before. Now it turned out his dad had a helicopter. A real-life helicopter! Wow!

"Here's your essay, son. I hope that's OK. And I realised I forgot to give you your dinner money. Here's £500."

Mr Spud pulled out a wad of crisp new £50 notes from his zebra-skin wallet. Joe pushed the money away, as all the other kids looked on in envy.

"Shall I pick you up at 4pm son?" asked Mr Spud.

"It's OK, thanks, Dad, I'll just get the bus," muttered Joe, looking down at the ground.

"You can pick *me* up in your helicopter, mate!" said one of the older boys.

"And me!" shouted another.

"And me!"

"Me!"

"ME!!"

"PICK ME!!!"

Soon all the kids in the playground were shouting and waving to get this short, fat, gold-jumpsuited man's attention.

Mr Spud laughed. "Maybe you can invite some of your friends over at the weekend and they can all have a helicopter ride!" he pronounced with a smile.

A huge cheer echoed around the playground.

"But Dad..." That was the last thing Joe wanted. For everyone to see how monstrously expensive their house was and how much crazy stuff they owned. He checked his plastic digital watch. He had less than 30 seconds to go.

"Dad, I gotta run," blurted out Joe. He snatched the essay out of his father's hands and raced into the main school building as fast as his short fat legs would take him.

Running up the staircase, he raced past the unfeasibly old headmaster, who was making his way down on a Stannah Stairlift. Mr Dust looked at least 100 years old, but was probably older. He was more suited to being an exhibit in the Natural History Museum than administrating a school, but he was harmless enough.

"Walk, don't run!" he mumbled. Even very old teachers are fond of catchphrases.

Hurling himself along the corridor to the classroom where Miss Spite was waiting, Joe realised half the school was following him. He even heard someone shout, "Hey, Bumfresh Boy!"

Unnerved, he pushed on, bursting into the classroom. The witch was holding her watch in her hand.

"I've got it, Miss Spite!" proclaimed Joe.

"You are five seconds late!" she proclaimed.

"You have got to be kidding Miss!" Joe couldn't believe anyone could be so mean. He glanced back behind him and saw hundreds of pupils were staring at him through the glass. Such was the eagerness to catch a glimpse of the richest boy in the school, or perhaps even the world, noses were pushed up against the glass so they looked like a tribe of pig-children.

"Litter duty!" said Miss Spite.

"But Miss—"

"A week's litter duty!"

"Miss—"

"One month's litter duty!"

Joe decided to say nothing this time and sloped across the classroom. He closed the door behind him. In the corridor hundreds of little pairs of eyes were still staring at him.

"Oi! Billionaire Boy!" came a deep voice from the back. It was one of the older boys, but Joe couldn't tell which one. In the sixth form *all* the boys had moustaches and Ford Fiestas. All the little mouths laughed.

"Lend us a million quid!" someone shouted. The laughter was now deafening. The noise clouded the air.

My life is officially over, thought Joe.

10

Dog Spit

As Joe scurried across the playground to the dining room, all the other kids swarmed around him. Joe kept his head down. He didn't like this instant superstardom at all. Voices whirled around him.

"Hey, Bum Boy! I'll be your best friend!"

"My bike got nicked. Buy us a new one mate."

"Lend us a fiver…"

"Let me be your bodyguard!"

"Do you know Justin Timberlake?"

"Me granny needs a new bungalow, give us a hundred grand will ya?"

"How many helicopters have you got?"

"Why do you bother going to school anyway, you are **rich!**"

"Can I have your autograph?"

"Why don't you have a massive party at yours on Saturday night?"

"Can I have a lifetime's supply of bog rolls?"

"Why don't you buy the school and sack all the teachers?"

"Can't you just buy me a bag of Maltesers? All right then, one Malteser? You are sooo mean!"

Joe started running. The crowd started running too. Joe slowed down. The crowd slowed down too. Joe turned and walked in the other direction. The crowd turned and walked in the other direction.

A little ginger-haired girl tried to grab his bag, and he thumped her hand away with his fist.

"Ow! My hand is probably broken," she cried. "I am going to sue you for ten million pounds!"

"Hit me!" said another voice.

"No me! Hit me!" said another.

A tall boy with glasses had a better idea. "Kick me in the leg and we can settle out of court for two million! Please?"

Joe sprinted into the school dining room. That was one place that was guaranteed to be empty at lunchtime. Joe struggled to force the double doors back on the tsunami of schoolchildren, but it was no use. They burst through, flooding the room.

"FORM AN ORDERLY QUEUE!" shouted the dinner lady, Mrs Trafe. Joe walked up to the serving counter.

"Now what would you like today, young Joe?" she said with a warm smile. "I have a very stinging nettle soup to start today."

"I am not that hungry today, maybe I'll go straight to a main course Mrs Trafe."

"It's chicken breast."

"Ooh, that sounds nice."

"Yes it comes in a dog spit sauce. Or for vegetarians I have deep fried Blu-tack."

Joe gulped. "Mmm, it's so hard to decide. See, I had some dog spit only last night."

"That's a shame. I'll give you a plate of the fried Blu-Tack then," said the dinner lady, as she dumped a lump of something blue and greasy and vomit-inducing on to Joe's plate.

"If you ain't having lunch then get out!" cried Mrs Trafe at the crowd still cowering at the doors.

"Spud's dad has got a helicopter Mrs Trafe," came a voice from the back.

"He's super-rich!" came another.

"He's changed!" came a third.

"Just give me a dead arm, Spud, and I will take a quarter of a million," came a tiny voice from the back.

"I SAID OUT!" shouted Mrs Trafe. The crowd reluctantly retreated, and contented themselves with staring at Joe through the grimy windows.

With his knife he removed the batter from the blue lump underneath. Now that raw potato seemed like food of the gods. After a few moments Mrs Trafe limped over to his table.

"Why are they all staring at you like that?" she asked kindly, as she slowly slumped her heavy frame down next to him.

"Well, it's a long story Mrs Trafe."

"You can tell me, pet," said Mrs Trafe. "I'm a school dinner lady. I reckon I've heard it all."

"Right, well..." Joe finished chewing the large lump of Blu-Tack he had in his mouth, and told the old dinner lady everything. About how his father had invented 'Bumfresh', how they now lived in a massive mansion, how they once had an orang-utan as a butler (she was very jealous of that bit), and how no one would have guessed a thing had his stupid dad not landed his stupid helicopter in the playground.

All the time he talked, the other kids continued to stare through the windows at him like he was an animal in the zoo.

"I am so sorry, Joe," said Mrs Trafe. "It must

be awful for you. You poor thing. Well not *poor* exactly, but you know what I mean."

"Thank you Mrs Trafe." Joe was surprised anyone would ever feel sorry for someone who had everything. "It's not easy. I don't know who to trust any more. All the kids in the school seem to want something from me now."

"Yeah, I bet," said Mrs Trafe, bringing out an M&S sandwich from her bag.

"You bring a packed lunch?" asked Joe, surprised.

"Oh yes, I wouldn't eat this filth. It's disgusting," she said. Her hand crept across the table and rested on his.

"Well, thanks for listening Mrs Trafe."

"That's OK, Joe. I am here for you anytime. You know that – anytime." She smiled. Joe smiled too. "Now…" said Mrs Trafe. "I just need ten thousand quid for a hip replacement…"

11

Camping Holiday

"You missed a bit," said Bob.

Joe bent down and picked up another piece of litter from the playground and put it in the bin liner Miss Spite had so generously provided. It was five o'clock now and the playground was empty of children. Only their litter remained.

"I thought you said you were going to help me," accused Joe.

"I am helping you! There's another bit." Bob pointed to another sweet wrapper that was lying on the asphalt, as he munched a bag of crisps. Joe bent down to pick it up. It was a Twix wrapper.

Probably the one he himself had dropped on the ground earlier that day.

"Well I guess everyone knows how rich you are now, Joe," said Bob. "Sorry about that."

"Yeah, I guess so."

"I suppose now all the kids at the school are going to want to be your friend..." said Bob, quietly. When Joe looked at him, Bob turned away.

"Maybe," Joe smiled. "But it means more that we were friends before everyone knew."

Bob grinned. "Cool," he said. Then he pointed to the ground at his feet. "You missed another bit there, Joe."

"Thanks, Bob," sighed Joe, as he bent down again, this time to pick up the crisp packet his friend had just dropped.

"Oh, no," said Bob.

"What's the matter?"

"Grubbs!"

"Where?"

"Over by the bike shed. What do they want?"

Lurking behind the shed were the twins. When they spotted Joe and Bob, they waved.

"I don't know what was worse," continued Bob. "Being bullied by them or being invited around for tea."

"HELLO, BOB!" shouted one Grubb, as they started lolloping towards them.

"Hello, Grubbs," Bob called back wearily.

Inexorably, the two bullies reached where the two boys were standing.

"We have been thinking," continued the other. "We are going on a camping trip at the weekend. Would you like to come?"

Bob looked at Joe for help. A camping holiday with these two was not an inviting invitation.

"Oh, what a terrible shame," said Bob. "I am busy this weekend."

"Next weekend?" asked Grubb one.

"That one too, I'm afraid."

"The one after that?" asked the other.

"Completely..." stammered Bob, "...chock full of things I've got to do. So sorry. It sounds so much fun. Anyway, see you two tomorrow, sorry, I would love to chat but I have to help Joe with his litter duty. Bye!"

"Any weekend next year?" asked the first Grubb.

Bob stopped. "Um... er... um... next year is, really busy for me. So I'd really really love to but I am so so sorry..."

"How about the year after?" asked Grubb Two. "Any free weekends? We have a lovely tent."

Bob couldn't keep it in any longer. "Look.

One day you're bullying me, the next you are inviting me to spend the weekend with you in a tent! What on earth is going on?"

The Grubbs looked to Joe for help. "Joe?" said one of them.

"We thought it would be easy being nice to Blob," said the other. "But he just says no to everything. What do you want us to do, Joe?"

Joe coughed, not very subtly. But the Grubbs didn't seem to get the hint.

"You paid them not to bully me, didn't you?" demanded Bob.

"No," replied Joe unconvincingly.

Bob turned to the Grubbs. "*Did* he?" he demanded.

"Noyes..." said the Grubbs. "We mean yesno."

"How much did he pay you?"

The Grubbs looked at Joe for help. But it was too late. They were all busted.

"Ten pounds each," said a Grubb. "And we *saw* the helicopter, Spud. We're not stupid. We want more cash."

"Yeah!" continued the other. "And you're

going in the bin, Joe, unless you give us eleven pounds each. First thing tomorrow."

The Grubbs stomped off.

Bob's eyes filled with angry tears. "You think money is the answer to everything don't you?"

Joe was baffled. He had paid off the Grubbs to *help* Bob. He was utterly perplexed as to why his friend was so upset. "Bob, I was just trying to help you, I didn't—"

"I am not some charity case, you know."

"I know that, I was just…"

"Yes?"

"I just didn't want to see you put in the bin again."

"Right," said Bob. "So you thought it would be better if the Grubbs were really weird and friendly and going on about camping trips."

"Well, they sort of came up with the camping trip on their own. But yes."

Bob shook his head. "I can't believe you. You're such a... such a... spoiled brat!"

"What?" said Joe. "I was just helping you out! Would you really rather be put in the bin and have your chocolate stolen?"

"Yes!" shouted Bob. "Yes, I would! I'll fight my own battles, thank you!"

"Suit yourself," said Joe. "Have fun being dumped in the bin."

"I will," replied Bob before storming off.

"Loser!" shouted Joe, but Bob didn't turn back.

Joe stood alone. A sea of litter surrounded him. He stabbed at a Mars wrapper with his litter stick. He couldn't believe Bob. He thought he'd found a friend, but all he'd really found was a selfish, bad tempered, ungrateful... *Ploomfizz*.

12

Page 3 Stunna

"… and the Witch still made me do litter duty!" said Joe. He was sitting with his dad at one end of the highly polished thousand-seater dining-room table waiting for his dinner. Impossibly large diamond candelabras hung overhead, and paintings that weren't very nice but cost millions of pounds adorned the walls.

"Even after I dropped your homework off in the chopper?" said Mr Spud, angrily.

"Yeah, it was so unfair!" replied Joe.

"I did not invent a double sided moist/dry toilet tissue for my son to be put on litter duty!"

"I know," said Joe. "That Miss Spite is such a cow!"

"I am going to fly to the school tomorrow and give that teacher of yours a piece of my mind!"

"Please don't, Dad! It was embarrassing enough when you turned up today!"

"Sorry, son," said Mr Spud. He looked a little hurt, which made Joe feel guilty. "I was just trying to help."

Joe sighed. "Just don't do it again, Dad. It's so awful everyone knowing I am the son of the Bumfresh man."

"Well, I can't help that, boy! That's how I made all this money. That's why we are living in this big house."

"Yeah… I guess," said Joe. "Just don't come turning up in your Bum Air helicopter or anything, yeah?"

"OK," said Mr Spud. "So, how's that friend

of yours working out?"

"Bob? He's not really my friend any more," replied Joe. He hung his head a little.

"Why's that?" asked Mr Spud. "I thought you and him were getting on really well?"

"I paid off these bullies to help him," said Joe. "They were making his life a misery, so I gave them some cash to leave him alone."

"Yeah, so?"

"Well, he found out. And then, get this, he got all upset. He called me a spoiled brat!"

"Why?"

"How do I know? He said he'd rather get bullied than have me help him."

Mr Spud shook his head in disbelief. "Bob sounds a bit of a fool to me. The thing is, when you've got money like we do, you meet a lot of ungrateful people. I reckon you're better off without this Bob character. It sounds like he doesn't understand the importance of money. If he wants to be miserable, let him."

"Yeah," agreed Joe.

"You'll make another friend at school, son," said Mr Spud. "You're rich. People like that. The sensible ones, anyway. Not like this idiot Bob."

"I'm not so sure," said Joe. "Not now everyone knows who I am."

"You will Joe. Trust me," said Mr Spud with a smile.

The immaculately attired butler entered the dining room through the vast oak panelled double doors. He did a little theatrical cough to get his master's attention. "Miss Sapphire Stone, gentlemen."

Mr Spud swiftly put on his ginger toupee as Page 3 stunna Sapphire clip-clopped into the room in her impossibly high heels.

"Sorry I'm late, I was just at the tanning

salon," she announced.

This was evident. Sapphire had fake tan smeared over every inch of her skin. She was now orange. As orange as an orange, if not orangier. Think of the orangiest person you've ever met, then times their orangeness by ten. As if she didn't look frightful enough already, she was wearing a lime green mini-dress and clutching a shocking pink handbag.

"What's *she* doing here?" demanded Joe.

"Be nice!" mouthed Dad.

"Nice pad," said Sapphire, looking round admiringly at the paintings and chandeliers.

"Thank you. It's just one of my seventeen homes. Butler, please tell Chef that we want our dinner now. What are we having tonight?"

"Foie gras, Sir," replied the butler.

"What's that?" asked Mr Spud.

"Specially fattened goose liver, Sir."

Sapphire grimaced. "I'll just have a bag of crisps."

"Me too!" said Joe.

"And me!" said Mr Spud.

"Three packets of potato crisps coming right up, Sir," sneered the butler.

"You look beautiful tonight, my angel!" said Mr Spud, before approaching Sapphire for a kiss.

"Don't smudge me lip liner!" said Sapphire, as she repelled him forcefully with her hand.

Mr Spud was clearly a little hurt, but tried to hide it. "Please take a seat. I see you brought the new Dior handbag I sent you."

"Yeah, but this bag comes in eight colours," she complained. "One for each day of the week. I thought you were gonna buy me all eight."

"I will, my sweet princess…" spluttered Mr Spud.

Joe stared at his dad. He couldn't believe he

had fallen for such a wrong'un.

"Dinner is served," announced the butler.

"Here, my beautiful angel of love, take a seat," said Mr Spud, as the butler pulled out a chair for her.

Three waiters entered the room carrying silver trays. They carefully placed the plates down on the table. The butler nodded and the waiters lifted the silver covers to reveal three packets of Salt n' Vinegar crisps. The trio started eating. Mr Spud initially attempted to eat his crisps with his knife and fork to appear posh, but soon gave up.

"Now me birfday's only eleven months away," said Sapphire. "So I've made a little wish-list of presents you are going to buy me…"

Her fingernails were so long and fake she could barely fish the piece of paper from her pink handbag. It was like watching one of those grabber machines at the fair where you never win anything. Eventually she grasped it and passed it over to Mr Spud. Joe looked over his dad's shoulder and read what she had scribbled.

Sapphire's Birfday Wish-list

A solid gold Rolls Royce convertible

A million pounds in cash

500 pairs of Versace sunglasses

A holiday home in Marbella (large)

A bucket of diamonds

A unicorn

A box of Ferrero Rocher chocolates (large)

A great big massive like really big yacht

A large tank of topical fish*

'Beverly Hills Chihuahua' on DVD

*I think she must mean tropical fish, rather than fish that are up on the news and current affairs.

5000 bottles of Chanel perfume

Another million pounds in cash

Some gold

Lifetime subscription to *OK* magazine

A private jet (new please, not second-hand)

A talking dog

General expensive stuff

100 designer dresses (I don't mind which ones as long as they are expensive. Any ones I don't like me mum can flog down the market)

A pint of semi-skimmed milk

Belgium

"Of course I will get all these things for you, my angel sent from heaven," slobbered Mr Spud.

"Thanks, Ken," said Sapphire, her mouth full of crisps.

"It's Len," corrected Dad.

"Oh, sorry, yeah! LOL! Len! Silly me!" she said.

"You can't be serious!" said Joe. "You're not really going to buy her all that stuff are you?"

Mr Spud gave Joe an angry look. "Why not, son?" he said, trying to control his temper.

"Yeah, why not, you little git?" said Sapphire. Definitely not controlling *her* temper.

Joe hesitated for a moment. "It's plain to see you're only with my dad for the money."

"Don't talk to your mother like that!" shouted Mr Spud.

Joe's eyes nearly popped out of his head. "She's not my *mother*, she's your stupid girlfriend and she's only seven years older than me!"

"How dare you!" fumed Mr Spud. "Say sorry."

Joe defiantly remained silent.

"I said, 'say sorry'!" shouted Mr Spud.

"No!" shouted Joe.

"Go to your rooms!"

Joe pushed back his chair, making as much of a clatter as possible, and stomped upstairs, as the staff pretcnded not to see.

He sat on the edge of his bed and cradled himself in his arms. It was a long, long time since anyone had hugged him, so he hugged himself. He squeezed his own sobbing plumpness. He was beginning to wish that Dad had never invented 'Bumfresh' and they were all still living in the council flat with Mum. After a few moments, there was a knock on the door. Joe sat in defiant silence.

"It's your dad."

"Go away!" shouted Joe.

Mr Spud opened the door and sat down next to his son on the bed. He nearly slid off the bedspread onto the floor. Silk sheets may look nice, but they aren't very practical.

Mr Spud bumjumped a little nearer to his son.

"I don't like to see my little Spud like this. I know you don't like Sapphire, but she makes me happy. Can you understand that?"

"Not really," said Joe.

"And I know you had a tough day at school too. With that teacher, the Witch, and with that ungrateful boy, Bob. I'm sorry. I know how much you wanted a friend, and I know I didn't make it any easier. I will have a quiet word with the headmaster. Try and sort things out for you if I can."

"Thanks, Dad." Joe sniffed. "I'm sorry I was crying." He hesitated for a moment. "I do love you, Dad."

"Ditto, son, ditto," replied Mr Spud.

13

New Girl

The half-term holidays came and went, and when Joe returned to school on the Monday morning he found he wasn't the centre of attention any more. There was a new girl at school, and because she was soooooooo pretty everyone was talking about her. When Joe walked into his classroom there she was, like a giant unexpected present.

"So what's the first lesson today?" she asked as they walked across the playground.

"Sorry?" spluttered Joe.

"I said, 'what's the first lesson today?'"

the new girl repeated.

"I know, it's just... you're really talking to me?" Joe couldn't believe it.

"Yes, I am talking to you," she laughed. "I'm Lauren."

"I know." Joe wasn't sure if the fact that he had remembered her name made him sound suave or like a stalker.

"What's your name?" she asked.

Joe smiled. At last there was someone at the school who knew nothing about him.

"My name is Joe," he said to Lauren.

"Joe what?" asked Lauren.

Joe didn't want her to know that he was the Bumfresh billionaire. "Erm, Joe Potato."

"Joe Potato?" she asked, more than a little surprised.

"Yes..." stammered Joe. In the moment he had been too overwhelmed by her beauty to be able to come up with a better alternative to 'Spud'.

"Unusual name, Potato," said Lauren.

"Yes, I suppose it is. It is actually spelt with an 'e' at the end. Joe *Potatoe*. So it's not quite the vegetable 'potato'. That would be ridiculous! Ha ha!"

Lauren tried to laugh too, but she was looking at Joe a little oddly. *Oh no*, thought Joe. *I only met this girl one minute ago and she already thinks I'm nuts.* He quickly tried to change the subject. "We've got Maths next with Mr Crunch," he said.

"OK."

"And then we've got History with Miss Spite."

"I hate History, it's so boring."

"You'll hate it even more with Miss Spite. She's a good teacher, I suppose, but all us kids

hate her. We call her 'The Witch'!"

"That's so funny!" said Lauren, giggling.

Joe felt ten feet tall.

Bob bobbed into view. "Er… Hi Joe."

"Oh, hi Bob," Joe replied. The two former friends hadn't seen each other over the half term. Joe had spent his days alone racing around and around his racetrack in a new Formula One car his dad had bought him. And Bob had spent most of the week in a bin. Wherever Bob was the

Grubbs seemed to find him, lift him up by his ankles and deposit him in the nearest skip. Well, that *was* what Bob had said he wanted.

Joe had missed Bob, but this wasn't good timing. Right now he was talking to the prettiest girl in the school, maybe even the prettiest girl in the whole of the local area!

"I know we haven't seen each other in a while. But… well… I've been thinking about what we said when you were doing litter duty…" stammered Bob.

"Yeah?"

Bob seemed a little taken aback by Joe's impatient tone, but pressed on. "Well, I am sorry we fell out, and I would like us to be friends again. You could move your desk back so that—"

"Do you mind if I talk to you later, Bob?" said Joe. "I am quite busy right now."

"But—" began Bob, a wounded expression on his face.

Joe ignored it. "I'll see you around," he said.

Bob marched off ahead.

"Who was that? A friend of yours?" enquired Lauren.

"No no no, he's not my friend," replied Joe. "Bob's his name, but he's so fat everyone calls him 'Blob'!"

Lauren laughed again. Joe felt a tiny bit sick, but he was so pleased to be making the pretty new girl laugh that he pushed the feeling all the way down inside him.

For the duration of the maths class Lauren kept on looking over at Joe. It put him right off his algebra. In History she was definitely gazing in his direction too. As Miss Spite droned on and on about the French revolution, Joe started to daydream about kissing Lauren. She was so very pretty that Joe wanted to kiss her more than anything. However, being only twelve Joe had never kissed a girl before, and had no idea how to make it happen.

"And the name of the king of France in 1789 was…? Spud?"

"Yes, Miss?" Joe stared at Miss Spite, horrified. He hadn't been listening at all.

"I asked you a question, boy. You haven't been paying attention, have you? Do you want to pass your exam?"

"Yes, Miss. I was listening…" stammered Joe.

"What is the answer then, boy?" demanded Miss Spite. "Who was the king of France in 1789?"

Joe had no idea. He was pretty sure it wasn't King Kevin II, or King Craig IV, or King Trevor the Great, because kings didn't tend to have names like that.

"I am waiting," pronounced Miss Spite. The bell rang. *I'm saved!* thought Joe.

"The bell is a signal for me, not you!" pronounced Miss Spite. Of course she was going to say that. She lived to say that. It would probably be written on her tombstone. Lauren was sitting behind where Miss Spite was standing, and she suddenly waved at Joe to get his attention. He was confused for a moment, then realised she was trying to help him by miming the answer. First she acted out someone going to the bathroom.

"King Toilet the…?" offered Joe.

The class all burst out laughing. Lauren shook her head. Joe had another try. "King Lavatory?"

They laughed again.

"King Bog?"

They laughed even harder this time.

"King Loo…? Ah, King Louis the…"

"Yes, boy?" Miss Spite continued her interrogation. Behind her Lauren mimed numbers with her fingers.

"King Louis the fifth, the tenth, the fifteenth, sixteen! King Louis the sixteenth!" declared Joe.

Lauren mimed a little clap.

"That's right, Spud," said a suspicious Miss Spite, before turning to the board and writing on it. "King Louis the sixteenth."

Stepping out into the spring sunshine, Joe turned to Lauren. "You totally saved my butt in there."

"That's OK. I like you." She smiled.

"Really…?" asked Joe.

"Yes!"

"Well, then, I wonder if…" Joe stumbled over his words. "If, well…"

"Well, what…?"

"If you, well, I mean you probably wouldn't,

in fact you definitely wouldn't, I mean, why would you? You are so pretty and I am just a big lump, but…" The words were spiralling out of his mouth in all directions now, and Joe was beginning to blush fiercely with embarrassment. "Well, if you wanted to…"

Lauren took over the speaking for a bit. "If I wanted to go for a walk in the park after school and maybe grab an ice lolly? Yes, I would love to."

"*Really*?" Joe was incredulous.

"Yes, really."

"With me?"

"Yes, with you, Joe Potatoe."

Joe was a hundred times happier than he could ever remember. It didn't even matter that Lauren thought his last name was Potatoe.

14

The Shape of a Kiss

"Oi!"

It had all been going perfectly. Joe and Lauren had been sitting on a park bench eating their lollies from Raj's shop. Raj could see Joe was trying to impress this girl, and so made a ridiculous fuss of him, giving him a one-penny discount on their lollies, and offering Lauren a free browse of *Now* magazine.

At last, though, they had escaped the newsagent's shop and found a quiet corner of the park, where they had been talking and talking as the melted red goo of their lollies dribbled down their fingers. They spoke about everything except Joe's family life. Joe didn't want to lie to Lauren. He already liked her too much for that. So when she asked him what his parents did he just told her his dad worked in 'human waste management' and unsurprisingly Lauren didn't enquire any further. Joe desperately didn't want Lauren to know how ridiculously rich he was. Having observed how Sapphire shamelessly used his dad, he knew only too well how money could ruin things.

Everything was perfect… until the sound of that "Oi!" spoiled everything.

The Grubb twins had been hanging around by the swings aching for someone to tell them off. Unfortunately for them, the police, the park-keeper and the local vicar were all otherwise engaged. So when one of them spotted Joe they bounced over grinning, no doubt hoping to relieve their boredom by making someone else's life a misery for a bit.

"Oi! Give us some more money or we'll put you in a bin!"

"Who are they talking to?" whispered Lauren.

"Me," said Joe reluctantly.

"Money!" said a Grubb. "Now!"

Joe reached into his pocket. Maybe if he gave them each a £20 note they would leave him alone, for today at least.

"What are you doing, Joe?" asked Lauren.

"I just thought…" he stammered.

"What's it to you, slag?" said Grubb One.

Joe looked down at the grass, but Lauren handed Joe what was left of her lolly and rose from the bench. The Grubbs shifted around uneasily. They weren't expecting a thirteen-year-old girl to literally stand up to them.

"Sit down!" said Grubb Two, as he or she put his or her hand on Lauren's shoulder to force her down onto the bench. Lauren, however, grabbed his or her hand and twisted it behind his or her back, and then pushed him or her to the ground. The other Grubb charged her, so Lauren leaped into the air and kung-fu kicked him or her to the ground. Then the other

one leaped up and tried to grab her, but she karate-chopped him or her on his or her shoulder and he or she raced off screaming in pain.

It really is quite hard writing this when you don't know someone's gender.

Joe felt it was about time he did something so he stood up and, his legs shaking in fear, approached the Grubb. It was only then that Joe realised he was still holding two melting ice lollies. The remaining twin stood its ground for a moment, and then when Lauren stood behind Joe he or she ran off, whimpering like a dog.

"Where did you learn to fight like that?" said Joe, astounded.

"Oh, I've just done a few martial arts classes, here and there," replied Lauren, a little unconvincingly.

Joe reckoned he might have found his dream

girl. Not only could Lauren be his girlfriend, she could be his bodyguard too!

They walked through the park. Joe had walked through it many times before, but today it seemed more beautiful than ever. As the sunlight danced through the leaves on the trees on this Autumn afternoon, for a moment everything in Joe's life seemed perfect.

"I'd better head home," Lauren said, as they neared the gate.

Joe tried to hide his disappointment. He could have strolled round the park with Lauren forever.

"Can I buy you lunch tomorrow?" he asked.

Lauren smiled. "You don't have to buy me anything. I'd love to have lunch with you, though, but I'm paying, you understand?"

"Well, if you really want to," said Joe. Wow. This girl was too good to be true.

"What's the school canteen like?" said Lauren.

How could Joe find the words? "Um, well, it's… it's great if you are on a very strict diet."

"I love healthy food!" said Lauren. That wasn't quite what Joe meant, but it was the best place at school for a date as it was guaranteed to be quiet.

"See you tomorrow then," said Joe. He closed his eyes and made his lips the shape of a kiss. And waited.

"See you tomorrow Joe," said Lauren, before skipping off down the path. Joe opened his eyes and smiled. He couldn't believe it! He had nearly kissed a girl!

15

Nip and Tuck

There was something very peculiar about Mrs Trafe today. She looked the same but different. As Joe and Lauren approached the serving counter, Joe realised what had changed.

The loose skin on her face had been lifted.

Her nose was smaller.

Her teeth were capped.

The lines on her forehead had been erased.

Her eye bags had disappeared.

Her wrinkles had gone.

Her breasts were much, much bigger.

But she was still limping.

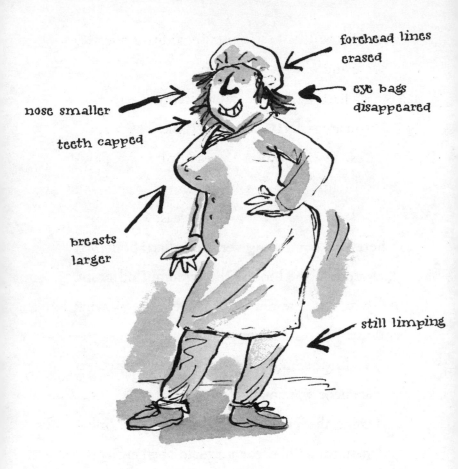

forehead lines
erased

eye bags
disappeared

nose smaller

teeth capped

breasts
larger

still limping

"Mrs Trafe, you look really… different…" Joe said, staring at her.

"Do I?" replied the old dinner lady with mock innocence. "Now, what do you two fancy today?

174

Roast bat with all the trimmings? Soap soufflé? Cheese and polystyrene pizza?"

"It's hard to choose…" faltered Lauren.

"You are new, are you, girl?" asked Mrs Trafe.

"Yes, I just joined the school yesterday," replied Lauren, surveying the dishes, and trying to work out which one was the least horrible.

"Yesterday? That's strange. I'm sure I've seen you somewhere before," said the dinner lady, studying Lauren's perfect face. "You look very familiar."

Joe butted in. "Did you have the hip replacement operation yet, Mrs Trafe?" He was becoming increasingly suspicious. "The one I gave you the money for a couple of weeks ago," he whispered, so Lauren wouldn't hear.

Mrs Trafe began to jabber nervously. "Um, well, no, not yet dear, why don't you have a large slice of my very tasty underpant flan…?"

"You spent the money I gave you on plastic surgery, didn't you?" hissed Joe.

A bead of sweat trickled down her face and plopped into her badger snot soup.

"I am sorry, Joe, I just, well, I just always wanted to have a few things done…" pleaded the dinner lady.

Joe was so furious he felt he had to leave instantly. "Lauren, we're going," he announced, and she followed as he stormed out of the dining room. Mrs Trafe limped after them.

"If you could just lend me another £5000, Joe, I promise I'll have it done this time!" she called after him.

When Lauren finally caught up with Joe, he was sitting alone in the far corner of the playground. She gently put her hand on his head to comfort him.

"What was all that about lending her £5000?" she asked.

Joe looked at Lauren. There was no way of avoiding telling her now. "My dad is Len Spud," he said sorrowfully. "'The Bumfresh billionaire'. My name's not Potatoe. I just said that so you wouldn't know who I was. The truth is, we're stupidly rich. But when people find out... it tends to ruin everything."

"You know what, some of the other kids told me this morning," said Lauren.

Joe's sadness lifted for a moment. He reminded himself that Lauren had still gone for an ice lolly with him yesterday when she thought he was just Joe. Maybe it wouldn't ruin things this time. "Why didn't you say anything?" he asked.

"Because it doesn't matter. I don't care about all that. I just like you," she said.

Joe was so happy he wanted to cry. It's strange how sometimes you can be so happy it goes all the way around to sadness. "I really like you too."

Joe moved closer to Lauren. This was the moment to kiss! He closed his eyes and pushed his lips together.

"Not here in the playground, Joe!" Lauren pushed him away laughing.

Joe felt embarrassed he had even tried. "I'm sorry." He quickly changed the subject. "I was just trying to do something kind for that old bag, and she goes and gets her knockers done!"

"I know, it's unbelievable."

"It's not the money, I don't care about the money…"

"No, it's that she took your generosity for granted," offered Lauren.

Joe looked up to meet her gaze. "Exactly!"

"Come on," said Lauren. "I think what you need is some chips. I'll buy you some."

The local chippy was bursting with kids from the comprehensive. It was against the rules to leave the school premises at lunchtime, but the food in the canteen was so abhorrent there wasn't much choice. The Grubbs were at the front of the queue, but fled as soon as they saw Lauren, leaving their battered sausages sizzling on the counter.

The pair stood outside on the pavement and ate their chips. Joe couldn't remember the last time he had enjoyed such a simple pleasure. It must have been when he was really, really little. Before the Bumfresh billions came and changed everything. Joe wolfed his chips down, and noticed Lauren had barely touched hers. He was still hungry, but wasn't sure whether their relationship had advanced to the point where he could start helping himself to her food. That was normally after a few years of marriage, and they weren't even engaged yet.

"Have you finished with yours?" he ventured.

"Yes," she replied. "I don't want to eat too much. I am working next week."

"Working? Doing what?" said Joe.

Lauren suddenly looked very flustered. "What did I say?"

"I thought you said you were working."

"Yeah yeah yeah, I *am* working." She paused, and then took a breath. "Just in a shop…"

Joe wasn't convinced. "So why would you

need to be thin to work in a shop?"

Lauren looked uncomfortable. "It's a very narrow shop," she said. She checked her watch. "We've got double Maths in ten minutes. We'd better go."

Joe frowned. There was something strange going on here…

16

Peter Bread

"The Witch is dead!" sang a spotty little boy. "Ding-dong, the wicked witch is dead!" It wasn't even registration time yet, but already the news was spreading across the school like flu.

"What do you mean?" asked Joe as he took his seat in his classroom. On the other side of the class, he could see Bob, looking over at him with a pained expression. *Probably jealous about Lauren*, thought Joe.

"Haven't you heard?" said another even spottier little boy behind him. "Spite's been sacked!"

"Why?" asked Joe.

"Who cares?!" said a slightly less spotty boy. "No more boring History lessons!"

Joe smiled, then frowned. He hated Miss Spite and her tedious lessons like everybody else, but wasn't sure she had done anything to deserve losing her job. Even though she was horrible, she was actually a good teacher.

"Spite's been sacked," blurted Joe to Lauren as she walked in.

"Yes, I heard," she replied. "It's brilliant news, isn't it?"

"Erm, well, I suppose so," said Joe.

"I thought that's what you wanted? You said you couldn't stand her."

"Yes, but…" Joe hesitated for a moment. "I just feel a bit, you know, sorry for her."

Lauren pulled a dismissive face.

Meanwhile, a gang of fierce-looking girls were

sat on desks at the back of the class. The smallest of the group was pushed over in Lauren's direction as the others looked on smirking.

"Got any Pot Noodles then?" she asked, much to the amusement of the gang.

Lauren shot a look at Joe. "I don't know what you mean," she protested.

"Don't lie," said the girl. "You look different in it, but I well reckon it's you."

"I have no idea what you're talking about," said Lauren, a little flustered.

Before Joe could speak a young man in old man's clothes entered the classroom and took his position uncertainly by the blackboard. "Simmer down please," he said quietly. No one in the classroom took any notice, except Joe.

"I said, 'simmer down please'…"

The new teacher's second sentence was barely more audible than the first. Still none of the other kids took any notice. In fact, if anything they started making even more noise than before.

"That's better," said the little man, trying to make the best of it. "Now, as you may know Miss Spite isn't here today—"

"Yeah, she's been given the boot!" shouted a loud fat girl.

"Well, that's not... well, yes, it is true..." the teacher continued in his faint monotone. "Now I am going to be taking over from Miss Spite as your form teacher, and also to teach you History and English. My name is Mr Bread." He began writing his name neatly on the board. "But you can call me Peter."

Suddenly there was quiet, as thirty little brains whirred.

"Pita Bread!" proclaimed a ginger-haired boy from the back. A huge wave of laughter crashed over the classroom. Joe had tried to give this poor man a chance, but he couldn't help but laugh.

"Please, please, can I have some quiet?" pleaded the unfortunately named teacher. But there was no use. The whole class was in uproar. The new form teacher had committed the biggest blunder any teacher can make – having a silly name. This is a serious point. If you have a name like any of those in the list below it is very, very important you don't become a teacher:

Sue Doku

Tom Atoe

Justin Case

Neil Down

Will Ing

Bob Head

Terry Daktul

Clare Voyant

Mel Formed

Rachel Prejudice

Mona Lott

Herbie Hind

Ima Hogg

Carol Singer

Dick Tate

Don Keigh

Rhoda Camel

Robin Banks

Felix Cited

Gerry Atrick

Bea O'Problem

Mya Bumreeks

Anita Bath

Sue Age

Marcus Absent

Al Gebra

Barbara Blacksheep

Kitty Litter

Mary Christmas

Jim Class

Doris Closed

Doris Locked

Wayne Dear

Dan Druff

Humphrey Dumpty

Stan Dupp

Cliff Hanger

Hugh Idiot

Lee King

Manuel Labour

Ruth Less

Willie Mammoth

Marsha Mellow

Walter Melon

Hazel Nut

Luke Out

Stu Pidd

Lolly Popp

Chuck Up

Seriously. Don't even consider it. The kids in your class will make your life a living hell.

Now, back to the story…

"Right," said the unfortunately named teacher. "I am going to take the register. Adams?"

"Don't forget Tara Mosalata!" shouted a skinny blonde-haired boy. The laughter swept up again.

"I did ask for quiet," said Mr Bread, pathetically.

"Or Ted Ziki!" hollered another kid. The laughter was deafening now.

Peter Bread put his head in his hands. Joe could almost feel sorry for him. This grey little man's life was going to be an utter misery from this day forward.

Oh, no, thought Joe. *We're all going to fail our exams.*

17

A Knock on the Toilet Door

There are a number of things you don't want to hear when you sit on the toilet.

A fire alarm.

An earthquake.

The roar of a hungry lion in the cubicle next door.

A large group of people shouting 'Surprise!' to you.

The sound of the entire toilet block being demolished by a giant wrecking ball.

The clicking sound of someone taking a photograph.

The sound of an electric eel swimming up the U-bend.

Someone drilling a hole in the wall.

JLS singing. (Admittedly that wouldn't be welcome at any time.)

A knock on the door.

That last one was exactly what Joe heard at break time when he took a seat in the boys' toilet.

RAT TAT TAT.

To be clear, that isn't a knock at *your* door, readers. It's a knock on Joe's toilet door.

"Who is it?" asked Joe, irritated.

"It's Bob," replied… yes, you've guessed correctly: Bob.

"Go away, I'm busy," said Joe.

"I need to talk to you."

Joe pulled the chain, and opened the door. "What do you want?" he said angrily as he made his way to the sink. Bob trailed after him munching on a bag of crisps. It was only an hour since he'd been eating chips like everyone else, but obviously Bob got hungry very easily.

"You shouldn't eat crisps in a toilet, Bob."

"Why not?"

"Because... because... I don't know, because the crisps wouldn't like it." Joe whacked the tap on to wash his hands. "Anyway, what do you want?"

Bob put the bag in his trouser pocket and stood behind his former friend. He looked into Joe's eyes in the mirror. "It's Lauren."

"What about her?" Joe had *known* it. Bob was just jealous.

Bob looked away for a second and took a deep breath. "I don't think you should trust her," he said.

Joe turned around, shaking with fury. "*What*

did you say?" he shouted.

Bob stepped away, taken aback. "I just think she's…"

"SHE'S WHAT?"

"She's fake."

"Fake?" Joe felt white-hot with fury.

"Lots of the other kids reckon she's an actress. They said she's in some advert, or something. And I saw her out with this other boy at the weekend."

"What?"

"Joe, I think she's just pretending to like you."

Joe put his face next to Bob's. He hated being this angry. It was scary being so out of control. "SAY THAT AGAIN…"

Bob backed away. "Look, I'm sorry, I don't want a fight, I am just telling you what I saw."

"You're lying."

"I'm not!"

"You're just jealous because Lauren likes me, and you're a fatty with no friends at all."

"I'm not jealous, I'm just worried for you, Joe. I don't want you to get hurt."

"Yeah?" said Joe. "You sounded really *worried about me* when you called me a spoiled brat."

"Honestly, I—"

"Just leave me alone, Bob. We're not friends any more. I felt sorry for you and talked to you and that was that."

"What did you just say? You felt 'sorry for me'?" Bob's eyes were wet with tears.

"I didn't mean…"

"What, because I'm fat? Because the other kids bully me? Because my dad's dead?" Bob was shouting now.

"No… I just… I didn't mean…" Joe didn't know what he meant. He reached into his pocket and pulled out a wad of £50 notes, and offered them to Bob. "Look, I'm sorry, here you go. Buy your mum something nice."

Bob knocked the money out of Joe's hand and the notes fell onto the damp floor. "How dare you?"

"What have I done now?" protested Joe. "What's the matter with you, Bob? I'm just trying to help you."

"I don't want your help. I don't want to ever speak to you again!"

"Fine!"

"And you are the one people should feel sorry for. You're pathetic." Bob stormed out.

Joe sighed, then got down on his knees and started picking up the wet bank notes.

"That's ridiculous!" said Lauren later, with a laugh. "I'm not an actress. I don't think I'd even get a part in the school play!"

Joe tried to laugh too, but he couldn't quite. They sat together on the bench in the playground, shivering slightly at the cold. Joe found it hard to say the next sentence. He did and didn't want to know the answer. He took a deep breath. "Bob said he saw you with some other boy. Is that true?"

"What?" said Lauren.

"At the weekend. He said he saw you out with someone else." Joe looked straight at her, trying to read her face. For a moment she seemed to retreat to the back of her eyes.

"He's a liar," she said after a moment.

"I thought so," said Joe, relieved.

"A big fat liar," she continued. "I can't believe you were ever friends with him."

"Well, it was only for a bit," squirmed Joe. "I don't like him anymore."

"I hate him. Lying pig. Promise me you won't ever speak to him again," said Lauren urgently.

"Well..."

"Promise, Joe."

"I promise," he replied.

A wicked wind whipped through the playground.

18

The Vortex 3000

Lauren didn't think the petition to get Miss Spite reinstated was going to be popular.

And she was right.

By the end of the day Joe had only got three signatures – his, Lauren's and Mrs Trafe's. The dinner lady had only signed it because Joe had agreed to try one of her Hamster Dropping Tartlets. It tasted worse than it sounded. Despite having what was essentially not much more than a blank sheet of paper, Joe still felt it was worth presenting his petition to the headmaster. He didn't like Miss Spite one bit, but he didn't understand why she had been sacked. Despite everything, she was a good teacher, certainly a lot better than Naan Bread, or whatever his stupid name was.

"Hello, children!" said the headmaster's secretary brightly. Mrs Chubb was a very fat jolly lady who always wore glasses with brightly coloured frames. She was always sitting in the headmaster's office behind her desk. In fact, no one had ever seen her stand up. It was not inconceivable that she was so big she was permanently wedged into her chair.

"We are here to see the headmaster, please," declared Joe.

"We have a petition for him," added a supportive Lauren, holding the piece of paper in her hand demonstratively.

"A petition! What fun!" beamed Mrs Chubb.

"Yes, it's to get Miss Spite her job back," said

Joe in a manly way that he hoped might impress Lauren. For a moment he toyed with the idea of thumping his fist on the desk to add emphasis, but he didn't want to topple over any of Mrs Chubb's abundant collection of lucky gonks.

"Oh, yes. Miss Spite, wonderful teacher. Don't understand that at all, but children I am sorry to say you have just missed Mr Dust."

"Oh, no," said Joe.

"Yes, he just left. Oh, look, there he goes." She pointed one of her bejewelled sausage fingers to the car park. Joe and Lauren peered through the glass. The headmaster was edging his way along at a snail's pace with his Zimmer frame.

"Slow down, Mr Dust, you'll do yourself a mischief!" she called after him. Then she turned back to Joe and Lauren. "He can't hear me. Well in truth he can't hear a thing! Do you want to leave that little petition thing with me?" She angled her head and studied it for a moment. "Oh dear, it looks like all the signatures have fallen off."

"We were hoping for more," said Joe, weakly.

"Well if you run you might just catch him!" said Mrs Chubb.

Joe and Lauren shared a smile, and walked slowly out to the car park. To their surprise Mr Dust had abandoned his Zimmer frame and was clambering astride a shiny new Harley Davidson motorbike. It was the brand new jet-powered Vortex 3000. Joe recognised it, because his dad had a small collection of 300 motorbikes and was always showing his son brochures of new ones he was going to buy. The superbike, at £250,000, was the most expensive motorbike ever produced. It was wider than a car, taller than a lorry, and blacker than a black hole. It shone with a very different chrome to that of the headmaster's Zimmer frame.

"Headmaster!" called Joe, but he was too late. Mr Dust had already put on his helmet and revved the engine. He put the beast into gear and

it roared past the other teachers' humble cars at a hundred miles an hour. It went so fast that the Headmaster was clinging on by his hands, his little old legs dangling up in the air behind him.

"YYYIIIıııPPPPPPPPPEEEEEEEEE.....!" cried the Headmaster as he and his preposterous machine disappeared off into the distance, becoming a dot on the horizon in a matter of seconds.

"There is something very strange going on," said Joe to Lauren. "The Witch gets the sack, the headmaster gets a £250,000 motorbike..."

"Joe, you're being silly! It's just coincidence!" laughed Lauren. "Now, am I still invited for dinner tonight?" she added, rapidly changing the subject.

"Yes yes yes," said Joe eagerly. "How about I meet you outside Raj's in an hour?"

"Cool. See you in a bit."

Joe smiled too, and watched her walk away.

But that bright golden glow that surrounded Lauren in Joe's mind was beginning to darken. Suddenly something felt very wrong...

19

A Baboon's Bottom

"Maybe your headmaster is simply having a mid-life crisis," pronounced Raj.

Stopping off at the newsagent's shop on the way home from school, Joe had told Raj about the curious events of the day.

"Mr Dust is about a hundred. He's got to be more than mid-way through his life!" said Joe.

"What I mean, Clever Clogs," continued Raj, "is that perhaps he was just trying to feel young again."

"But it's the most expensive motorbike in the world. It costs a quarter of a million pounds.

He's a teacher not a footballer, how could he afford it?!" proclaimed Joe.

"I don't know… I am no detective like Miss Marbles, or the great Shylock Holmes," said Raj, before looking around his shop and lowering his voice to a whisper. "Joe, I need to ask you about something in the strictest confidence."

Joe lowered his voice too. "Go ahead."

"This is very embarrassing, Joe," whispered Raj. "But do you use your dad's special toilet paper?"

"Yes, of course, Raj. Everybody does!"

"Well, I have been using his new one for a few weeks now."

"The mint-flavoured bum wipes?" asked Joe. There was now a huge range of Bumfresh products including:

HOTBUMFRESH – warms your bottom as you wipe.

LADYBUMFRESH – specially soft wipes for ladies' bottoms.

MINTYBUMFRESH – leaves your bottom with a cool, minty aroma.

"Yes, and…" Raj took a deep breath. "My bottom has come up all… well… purple."

"Purple!" said Joe with a shocked laugh.

"This is a very serious matter," chided Raj. He looked up suddenly. "One copy of the *Daily Mail* and a packet of Rolos, that will be 85p, be careful with those Rolos on your dentures, Mr Little."

He waited for the pensioner to leave the shop. *Ding* went the bell on the door.

"I didn't see him there. He must have been lurking behind the Quavers," said Raj, a little shaken at what the pensioner might have heard.

"You are joking aren't you, Raj?" said Joe with a quizzical smile.

"I am deadly serious, Joe," said Raj gravely.

"Show me, then!" said Joe.

"I can't show you my bottom Joe! We've only just met!" exclaimed Raj. "But let me draw you a simple graph."

"A graph?" asked Joe.

"Be patient, Joe."

As the boy looked on Raj grabbed some paper and pens and drew this simple graph.

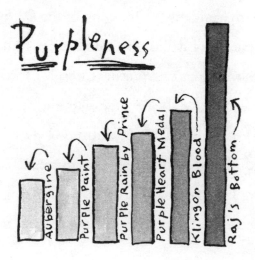

"Wow, that is purple!" said Joe, studying the graph. "Is it painful?"

"It is a little sore."

"Have you seen a doctor?" asked Joe.

"Yes, and he said he had seen hundreds of people in the local area with brightly coloured bottoms."

"Oh no," said Joe.

"Maybe I will have to have a bum transplant!"

Joe couldn't help but laugh. "A bum transplant?!"

"Yes! This isn't a laughing matter, Joe," chided Raj. There was hurt in his eyes that his bottom had become the subject of mockery.

"No, sorry," said Joe, still giggling.

"I think I will stop using your dad's new Bumfresh wipes and go back to the shiny white my wife used to buy."

"I'm sure it isn't the bum wipes," said Joe.

"What else could it be?"

"Look, Raj, I'd better go," Joe said. "I have invited my girlfriend over later."

"Oooh, girlfriend is it now? The pretty girl you came in with when I sold you the ice lollies?" said the newsagent brightly.

"Yes, that's her," said Joe shyly. "Well, I don't know if she really is my girlfriend, but we've been spending lots of time together..."

"Well, have a lovely evening!"

"Thanks." Arriving at the door Joe turned back to the newsagent. He couldn't help himself. "Oh, by the way, Raj, good luck with the bum transplant..."

"Thank you, my friend."

"I hope they can find one big enough!" Joe laughed.

"Out of my shop! Out! Out!" said Raj.

Ding.

"Cheeky boy," muttered the newsagent with a smile, as he rearranged his Curly Wurlys.

20

A Beach Ball Rolled in Hair

Bumfresh Towers pulsated with music. Coloured lights spun in every room. Hundreds of people swarmed around the house. This was a party that was going to get complaints about the noise.

From people in Sweden.

Joe had no idea that there was a party at the house tonight. Dad hadn't mentioned anything at breakfast and Joe had invited Lauren over for dinner. As it was a Friday night they could stay up late too. It was going to be perfect. Maybe tonight they might even kiss.

"Sorry, I had no idea about all this," said Joe,

as they approached the giant stone steps at the front of the house.

"It's cool, I love a party!" replied Lauren.

As darkness fell and strangers tumbled out of the house clutching bottles of champagne, Joe took Lauren's hand, and led her through the huge oak front door.

"Wow, this is some house," shouted Lauren over the music.

"What?" said Joe.

Lauren put her mouth to Joe's ear so she could be heard. "I said, 'wow, this is some house'." But Joe still couldn't really hear. Feeling the heat of her breath so close to him was so exhilarating he stopped listening for a moment.

"THANK YOU!" shouted Joe back into Lauren's ear. Her skin smelt sweet, like honey.

Joe searched all over the house for his dad. It was impossible to find him. Every room was oozing with people. Joe didn't recognise a single one of them. Who on earth were they all? Guzzling cocktails and gobbling finger food like there was no tomorrow. Being short, Joe really found it hard to see over them. His dad wasn't in the snooker room. He wasn't in the dining room. He wasn't in the massage room. He wasn't in the library. He wasn't in the other dining room. He wasn't in his bedroom. He wasn't in the reptile house.

"Let's try the pool room!" shouted Joe in Lauren's ear.

"You've got a pool! Cool!" she shouted back.

They passed a woman bent over vomiting by the sauna as a man (presumably her boyfriend) patted the small of her back supportively. Some party guests had either dived or fallen into the pool, and were bobbing around in the water. Joe enjoyed swimming, and the thought that none of these people looked like they would get out of the pool if they needed a pee, clouded his mind.

Just then he spotted his dad – wearing just a pair of swimming trunks and his curly afro toupee, and dancing to a completely different song than the one that was playing. Covering the wall behind him was a vast mural of a strangely muscle-bound version of himself reclining in a thong. The real Mr Spud boogied badly in front of it, looking more like a beach ball that had been rolled in hair.

"What's going on, Dad?" Joe shouted, half because the music was so loud and half because he was angry his dad hadn't told him anything about the party. "Who are all these people? Your friends?"

"Oh no, I hired them in. £500 each. Partyguests.com."

"What's the party for, Dad?"

"Well, I know you will be so pleased to know that Sapphire and I have got engaged!" shouted Mr Spud.

"What the—?" said Joe, not able to disguise his shock.

"It's great news isn't it?" Dad yelled. Still the music boom boom boomed.

Joe didn't want to believe it. Did this brainless bimbo really have to be his new mum?

"I asked her yesterday and she said 'no', but then I asked her again today and gave her a great big diamond ring and she said 'yes'."

"Congratulations, Mr Spud," said Lauren.

"So you must be a friend of my son's from school?" said Mr Spud, his words tumbling out clumsily.

"That's right, Mr Spud," replied Lauren.

"Call me Len, please," said Mr Spud with a smile. "And you must meet Sapphire. SAPPHIRE!" he shouted.

Sapphire tottered over in her shocking yellow high heels and even more shocking yellow mini-dress.

"Would you show Joe's friend the engagement ring, my gorgeous lady love of all time? Twenty million quid, just for the diamond."

Joe spied the diamond on his soon to be stepmother's finger. It was the size of a small bungalow. Her left arm was dangling lower than the right with the weight of it.

"Er... er... oh... It's so heavy, I can't lift my hand but if you bend down you can see it..." said Sapphire. Lauren stepped closer to get a better look. "Haven't I seen ya somewhere before?" Sapphire asked.

Mr Spud leaped in. "No, you haven't, my one true love."

"Yes I have!" said Sapphire.

"No, my angel cake!"

"OMG! I know where I seen ya!"

"I said shut it, my chocolate sprinkled princess!" said Mr Spud.

"You done that ad for Pot Noodle!" Sapphire exclaimed.

Joe turned to Lauren, who looked at the floor.

"It's well good, you know the one, Joe," continued Sapphire. "For the new sweet and sour flavour. The one where she has to do karate to stop people from nicking it!"

"You *are* an actress!" spluttered Joe. The advert was coming back into focus in his mind. Her hair was a different colour, and she wasn't wearing an all in one yellow catsuit, but it was Lauren all right.

"I better go," said Lauren.

"And did you lie about having a boyfriend too?" demanded Joe.

"Goodbye Joe," said Lauren, before weaving past the guests in the poolroom as she ran off.

"LAUREN!" shouted Joe after her.

"Let her go, son," said Mr Spud sadly.

But Joe raced after her, and caught up with her just as she reached the stone steps. He grabbed her arm, harder than he had anticipated and she turned around in pain.

"Oww!"

"Why did you lie to me?" Joe stammered.

"Just forget it, Joe," said Lauren. She suddenly seemed a different person. Her voice was more posh now and her face less kind. The twinkle in her eye had definitely gone, and the glow around her had turned into a shadow. "You don't want to know."

"Don't want to know what?"

"Look, if you must know your dad saw me on that Pot Noodle advert and called my agent. Said you were unhappy at school, and paid me to be your friend. It was all fine until you tried to kiss me."

She skipped down the steps and ran off down the long drive. Joe watched her go for a few moments, before the pain in his heart was so great he had to bend over to stop it. He fell to his knees. A party guest stepped over him. Joe didn't even look up. He felt he was so sad that he was never going to be able to get up again.

21

A GCSE in Make-Up

"DAD!" screamed Joe. He had never been this angry before, and hoped he never would be again. He ran into the pool room to confront his father.

Mr Spud nervously straightened his toupee as his son approached.

Joe stood in front of his dad hyperventilating. He was too angry to speak.

"I am sorry, son. I thought that's what you wanted. A friend. I just wanted to make things better for you at school. I got that teacher you hated sacked too. All I had to do was buy the headmaster a motorbike."

"So…. You got an old lady sacked from her job… And then, and then… you… paid a girl to like me…"

"I thought that's what you wanted."

"*What*?"

"Listen, I can buy you another friend," said Mr Spud.

"YOU DON'T GET IT DO YOU?" screamed Joe. "Some things can't be bought."

"Like what?"

"Like friendship. Like feelings. Like love!"

"Actually, that last one can," offered Sapphire, still unable to lift her hand.

"I hate you Dad, I really do," shouted Joe.

"Joe, please," pleaded Mr Spud. "Look, please calm down. How about a nice little cheque for five million quid?"

"Ooh, yes please," said Sapphire.

"I don't want any more of your stupid money," sneered Joe.

"But son…" spluttered Mr Spud.

"The last thing I want to do is end up like you… A middle-aged man with some brain-dead teenage fiancée!"

"Excuse me, I've got a GCSE in make-up," said Sapphire angrily.

"I never want to see either of you again!" said Joe. He ran out of the room, pushing the vomiting lady out of his way and into the pool as he did so. Then he slammed the huge door behind him. One of the mural tiles from Mr Spud's thong fell off the wall and smashed onto the floor.

"JOE! JOE! WAIT!" shouted Mr Spud.

Joe dodged past the hordes of guests and ran up to his room, shutting the door firmly behind him. There wasn't a lock, so he grabbed a chair and wedged it under the door handle so it wouldn't open. As the beat of the music thumped through the carpet, Joe grabbed a bag and started filling it with clothes. He didn't know where he was going, so wasn't sure what he needed. All he knew was that he didn't want to be in this ridiculous house for another minute. He grabbed a couple of his favourite books (*The*

Boy in the Dress and *Mr Stink*, both of which he found hilarious and yet heart-warming).

Then he looked on his shelf at all his expensive toys and gadgets. His eyes were drawn to the little loo-roll rocket that his dad had given him when he still worked at the factory. He remembered it was a present for his eighth birthday. His mum and dad were still together then and Joe thought it might have been the last time he was truly happy.

As his hand reached out to take it there was a loud thump on the door.

"Son, son, let me in…"

Joe didn't say a word. He had nothing more he wanted to say to the man. Whoever his dad had been was lost years ago.

"Joe, please," said Mr Spud. Then there was a pause.

TTTTHHHHHUUUUUMMMM
MPPPPP.

Joe's dad was trying to force the door open.

"Open this door!"

TTTTTTTTTTTTHHHH
HHHHHHHHHHHHH
HUUUUUUUUUUUM
MMMMMMMPPPPPPP
PPPP.

"I've given you everything!" He was putting all his weight behind it now, and the chair legs heroically dug themselves deeper into the carpet. He made one last try.

TTTTTTTTTTTTTT
TTHHHHHHHHHH
HHHHHHHHHHHH
HHHHUUUUUUUU

UUUUUUUMM MMMMMMMMM MMMMMMMPPPP PPPPPPPPPPPPPPP PPPPPPPPPPP.

Joe then heard a much smaller thump as his dad gave in and leaned his body against the door. This was followed by a squeak as his bulk slid down the door, and a few whimpering cries. Then the light in the gap under the door was blocked. His dad must have been slumped on the floor.

Spud Junior felt unbearably guilty. He knew all he needed to do to stop his dad's pain was open that door. He put his hand on the chair for a moment. *If I open that door now*, he thought, *nothing is going to change.*

Joe took a deep breath, lifted his hand, grabbed his bag and walked to the window. He opened it slowly so his dad wouldn't hear, and then climbed onto the windowsill. Joe took one last look at his bedroom before jumping out into the darkness, and a new chapter.

22

A New Chapter

Joe ran as fast as he could – which wasn't that fast, in all honesty. But it felt fast to him. He ran down the long, long drive. Dodged past the guards. Jumped over the wall. Was that wall to keep people out or keep him in? He'd never thought about it before. But there wasn't time to think about it now. Joe had to run. And keep running.

Joe didn't know where he was running to. All he knew was where he was running from. He couldn't live in that stupid house with his stupid dad for one moment longer. Joe ran down the road. All he could hear was his own breath, getting faster and faster. There was a faint taste of blood in his mouth. Now he wished he had tried harder in the school cross-country run.

It was late now. After midnight. The lamp posts pointlessly illuminated the empty little town. Reaching the town centre, Joe slowed to a stop. A lone car crouched in the road. Realising he was alone, Joe suddenly felt a shiver of fear. The reality of his great escape dawned on him. He looked at his reflection in the window of the darkened KFC. A chubby twelve-year-old boy with nowhere to go looked back at him. A police car rolled past slowly and silently. Was it looking for him? Joe hid behind the big plastic bin. The smell of fat and ketchup and hot cardboard was so stomach-churning it almost made him choke. Joe covered his mouth to stifle the sound. He didn't want the policemen to discover him.

The police car turned a corner and Joe ventured out into the street. Like a hamster that had escaped from its cage, he kept close to the edges and corners. Could he go to Bob's? *No*, thought Joe. In the exhilaration of meeting Lauren or whatever her stupid name really was, he had badly let down his only friend. Mrs Trafe had been a sympathetic ear, but it turned out she was after his money all along.

How about Raj? *Yes*, thought Joe. He could go and live with the purple-bottomed newsagent. Joe could set up camp behind the fridge. Hidden safely there, Joe could read *Nuts* magazine all day, and feast on slightly out of date confectionery. He couldn't imagine a more charmed life.

Joe's mind was racing, and soon his legs were too. He crossed the road and turned left. Raj's shop was only a few streets away now.

Somewhere above him in the black air he heard a distant whirr. The whirr became louder. More of a buzz. Then a drone.

It was a helicopter. A searchlight danced across the streets. Mr Spud's voice came out of a loudspeaker.

"JOE SPUD, THIS IS YOUR DAD SPEAKING. GIVE YOURSELF UP. I REPEAT, GIVE YOURSELF UP."

Joe dashed into the entrance of The Body Shop. The searchlight had just missed him. The smell of pineapple and pomegranate body wash and dragonfruit foot scrub pleasingly tickled its way up his nostrils. Hearing the helicopter passing overhead, Joe dashed to the other side of the street, and crept past Pizza Hut, and then Pizza Express, before seeking sanctuary in the doorway of a Domino's Pizza. Just as he stepped out to make a dash past Bella Pasta, the

helicopter whooshed back overhead. Suddenly
Joe Spud was caught in the dead centre of the
searchlight.

"DON'T MOVE. I REPEAT, DON'T
MOVE," the voice thundered.

Joe looked up into the light as his body trembled from the force of the rotor blades. "Shove off!" he shouted. "I repeat, shove off!"

"COME HOME NOW, JOE."

"No."

"JOE, I SAID..."

"I heard what you said and I'm not coming home. I'm not ever coming home," shouted Joe. Standing there in the bright light he felt like he was on stage in a particularly dramatic school play. The helicopter whirred overhead for a moment as the loudspeaker crackled in silence.

Then Joe made a run for it, dashing down an alley behind Argos, through the NCP car park, and round the back of Superdrug. Soon the helicopter was nothing more than a distant buzz, no louder than the sleepless birds.

Arriving at Raj's, Joe knocked gently on the metal shutters. There was no answer, so he banged this time until the shutters shook with the force of his fists. Still no answer. Joe looked at his watch. It was two o'clock in the morning. No wonder Raj wasn't in his shop.

It looked like Joe would have to be the very first billionaire to ever sleep rough.

23

Canal Boat Weekly

"What are you doing in there?"

Joe wasn't sure if he was awake, or simply dreaming that he was awake. He certainly couldn't move. His body felt stiff with cold, and every part of him ached. Joe couldn't open his eyes yet, but knew without doubt that he hadn't woken up between the silk sheets of his four-poster bed.

"I said, what are you doing in there?" came the voice again. Joe frowned, puzzled. His butler didn't have an Indian accent. Joe struggled to unglue eyes that had been stuck together with sleep. He saw a big smiley face hovering over his.

It was Raj's.

"Why are you here at this ungodly hour, Master Spud?" asked the kindly newsagent.

As dawn was beginning to glow through the gloom, Joe took in his surroundings. He had climbed into a skip outside Raj's shop and fallen asleep. Some bricks had been his pillow, a piece of tarpaulin his duvet, and a dusty old wooden door his mattress. No wonder every part of his body ached.

"Oh, er, hello Raj," croaked Joe.

"Hello Joe. I was just opening up my shop and heard some snoring. There you were. I was quite surprised, I must tell you."

"I don't snore!" protested Joe.

"I regret to inform you that you do. Now would you be so kind as to climb out of the skip and step inside my shop, I think we need to talk," said Raj, in a deadly serious tone.

Oh no, thought Joe, *now I'm in trouble with Raj.*

Although Raj was adult in age and size, he was nothing like a parent or a teacher, and it was really difficult to get into trouble with him. Once one of the girls from Joe's school had been caught trying to steal a bag of Wotsits from the newsagent and Raj had banned her from his shop for all of five minutes.

The dusty billionaire clambered out of the skip. Raj fashioned him a stool from a stack of *Heat* magazines, and wrapped a copy of the *Financial Times* over his shoulders like it was a big pink boring blanket.

"You must have been outside in the cold all night, Joe. Now, you must eat some breakfast. A nice hot mug of Lilt perhaps?"

"No thanks," said Joe.

"Two Rolo eggs, poached?"

Joe shook his head.

"You need to eat, boy. A toasted Galaxy bar?"

"No thanks."

"A hearty bowl of Pickled Onion Monster Munch perhaps? With warm milk?"

"I am really not hungry, Raj," said Joe.

"Well, my wife has put me on a strict diet so I am only allowed fruit for breakfast now," announced Raj as he unwrapped a Terry's Chocolate Orange. "Now, are you going to tell me why you slept in a skip last night?"

"I ran away from home," announced Joe.

"I guessed that much," slurred Raj, chewing away on multiple segments of Terry's Chocolate Orange. "Oooh, pips," he said before spitting something into the palm of his hand. "The question is, why?"

Joe looked ill at ease. He felt the truth shamed him as much as his dad. "Well you know that girl I brought in here the day we got some ice lollies?"

"Yes, yes! You know I said I had seen her

somewhere before? Well, she was on TV last night! On an advert for Pot Noodle Snacks! So did you finally kiss her?" exclaimed an excited Raj.

"No. She was only pretending to like me. My dad paid her to be my friend."

"Oh dear," said Raj. His smile fell from his face. "That's not right. That's not right at all."

"I *hate* him," said Joe hotly.

"Please don't say that, Joe," said Raj, shocked.

"But I do," said Joe, turning to Raj with fire in his eyes. "I hate his guts."

"Joe! You must stop talking like this right now. He is your father."

"I hate him. I never want to see him again for as long as I live."

Tentatively, Raj reached out and put his hand on Joe's shoulder. Joe's anger immediately turned to sadness, and with his head bowed he began to weep into his own lap. His body shook involuntarily as the waves of tears ebbed and flowed through him.

"I can understand your pain, Joe, I really can," ventured Raj. "I know from what you said that you really liked that girl, but I guess your dad was, well… just trying to make you happy."

"It's all that money," said Joe, barely audible through the tears. "It's ruined everything, I even lost my only friend over it."

"Yes, I haven't seen you and Bob together for a while. What happened?"

"I've behaved like an idiot too. I said some really mean things to him."

"Oh dear."

"We fell out when I paid some bullies to leave him alone. I thought I was helping him, but he got all angry about it."

Raj nodded slowly. "You know, Joe…" he

said slowly. "It doesn't sound as though what you did to Bob is so very different to what your father did to you."

"Maybe I am a spoiled brat," Joe told Raj. "Just like Bob said."

"Nonsense," said Raj. "You did a stupid thing, and you must apologise. But if Bob has any sense, he will forgive you. I can see that your heart was in the right place. You meant well."

"I just wanted them to stop bullying him!" Joe said. "I just thought, if I gave them money…"

"Well, that's no way to beat bullies, young man."

"I know that now," admitted Joe.

"If you give them money they'll just come back and back for more."

"Yes, yes, but I was only trying to help him."

"You have to realise money can't solve

everything, Joe. Maybe Bob would have stood up to the bullies himself, eventually. Money is not the answer! You know I was once a very rich man?"

"Really?!" said Joe, instantly embarrassed that he sounded a little too surprised. He sniffed and wiped his wet face on his sleeve.

"Oh, yes," replied Raj. "I once owned a large chain of newsagent shops."

"Wow! How many shops did you have, Raj?"

"Two. I was taking home literally hundreds of pounds a week. If I wanted anything I would simply have it. Six Chicken McNuggets? I would have nine! I splashed out on a flash brand new second-hand Ford Fiesta. And I would think nothing of returning a DVD to Blockbuster a day late and thus incurring a £2.50 fine!"

"So, um, yeah, that sounds like quite a rollercoaster ride," said Joe, not sure what else to say. "What went wrong?"

"Two shops meant I was working very long hours, young Joe, and I forgot to spend time with the one person I really loved. My wife. I would buy her lavish gifts. Boxes of After Eight mints, a gold-plated necklace from the Argos catalogue, designer dresses from George at Asda. I thought that was the way to make her happy, but all she really wanted was to spend time with me," concluded Raj with a sad smile.

"That's all I want!" exclaimed Joe. "To just spend time with my dad. I don't care about all the stupid money," said Joe.

"Come on, I am sure your father loves you very much, he'll be worried sick. Let me take you home," said Raj.

Joe looked at Raj and managed a little smile.

"OK. But can we stop off at Bob's on the way? I really need to talk to him."

"Yes, I think you are right. Now, I believe I have his address somewhere as his mum gets the *Mirror* delivered," said Raj as he began to flick through his address book. "Or is it the *Telegraph*? Or is it *Canal Boat Weekly*? I never can remember. Ah, here we are. Flat 112. The Winton Estate."

"That's miles away," said Joe.

"Don't worry, Joe. We will take the Rajmobile!"

24

The Rajmobile

"*This* is the Rajmobile?" asked Joe.

He and Raj were looking at a tiny girl's tricycle. It was pink and had a little white basket on the front and would have been too small for a girl of six.

"Yes!" said Raj proudly.

When Raj had mentioned the Rajmobile, Joe's mind had conjured up images of Batman's Batmobile or James Bond's Aston Martin, or at least Scooby Doo's van.

"It's a little small for you, don't you think?" he asked.

"I bought it on eBay for £3.50, Joe. It looked

a lot bigger in the photograph. I think they had a midget stand next to it in the picture! Still, at that price, quite a bargain."

Reluctantly, Joe sat in the basket at the front, as Raj took his place on the saddle.

"Hold on tight, Joe! The Rajmobile is quite a beast!" said Raj, before he started pedalling, and the trike trundled off slowly, squeaking with every turn of the wheels.

dr**ING**.

That wasn't... Oh, I think I've done that joke too many times now.

"Hello?" said a kindly but sad-looking lady at the door of Flat 112.

"Are you Bob's mum?" asked Joe.

"Yes," said the woman. She squinted at him. "You must be Joe," she said, in a not-very-friendly tone. "Bob has told me all about *you*."

"Oh," squirmed Joe. "I'd like to see him, if that's OK."

"I'm not sure he'll want to see you."

"It's really important," said Joe. "I know I've treated him badly. But I want to make up for it. Please."

Bob's mum sighed, then opened the door. "Come in then," she said.

Joe followed her into the little flat. The whole thing could have fitted into his en-suite bathroom. The building had definitely seen better days. Wallpaper was peeling off the walls, and the carpet was worn in places. Bob's mum led Joe along the corridor to Bob's room and knocked on his door.

"What?" came Bob's voice.

"Joe is here to see you," replied Bob's mum.

"Tell him to get lost."

Bob's mum looked at Joe, embarrassed.

"Don't be rude, Bob. Open the door."

"I don't want to talk to him."

"Maybe I should go?" whispered Joe, half turning towards the front door. Bob's mum shook her head.

"Open this door at once, Bob. You hear me? At once!"

Slowly the door opened. Bob was still in his pyjamas, and stood staring at Joe.

"What do you want?" he demanded.

"To talk to you," replied Joe.

"Go on then, talk."

"Shall I make you two some breakfast?" asked Bob's mum.

"No, he's not staying," replied Bob.

Bob's mum's tutted and disappeared into the kitchen.

"I just came to say I'm sorry," spluttered Joe.

"It's a bit late for that, isn't it?" said Bob.

"Look, I am so, so sorry for all the things I said."

Bob was defiant in his anger. "You were really nasty."

"I know, I'm sorry. I just couldn't work out why you were so upset with me. I only gave the Grubbs money because I wanted to make things easier for you—"

"Yes, but—"

"I know, I know," said Joe hurriedly. "I realise

now it was the wrong thing to do. I'm just explaining how I felt at the time."

"A true friend would have stuck up for me. Supported me. Instead of just flashing their money around to make the problem go away."

"I am an idiot, Bob. I know that now. A great big fat stinking idiot."

Bob smiled a little, though he was clearly trying hard not to.

"And you were right about Lauren, of course," continued Joe.

"About her being a fake?"

"Yes, I found out my dad was paying her to be my friend," said Joe.

"I didn't know that. That must have really hurt."

Joe's heart ached, as he remembered how much pain he had felt at the party last night. "It did. I really liked her."

"I know. You forgot who your *real* friends were."

Joe felt so guilty. "I know… I'm so sorry. I do really like you, Bob. I really do. You're the only kid at school who ever liked me for me, not just my money."

"Let's not fall out again. Eh Joe?" Bob smiled.

Joe smiled too. "All I ever really wanted was a friend."

"You're still my friend, Joe. You always will be."

"Listen," Joe said. "I've got something for you. A present. To say sorry."

"Joe!" said Bob, frustrated. "Look, if it's a new Rolex or a load of money I don't want it, all right?"

Joe smiled. "No, it's just a Twix. I thought we could share it."

Joe pulled out the chocolate bar and Bob

chuckled. Joe chuckled too. He opened the packet and handed Bob one of the fingers. But just as Joe was about to scoff the chocolate and caramel topped biscuit...

"Joe?" called Bob's mum from the kitchen. "You better come quickly. Your dad is on the TV..."

25

Broken

Broken. That's the only word that could describe how Joe's dad looked. He was standing outside Bumfresh Towers, in his dressing gown. Mr Spud addressed the camera, his eyes red from crying.

"I've lost everything," he said slowly, his whole face shattered with emotion. "Everything. But all I want is my son back. My beautiful boy."

Then the tears welled up in Mr Spud and he had to catch his breath.

Joe looked over at Bob and his mum. They stood in the kitchen staring at the screen. "What does he mean? He's lost everything?"

"It was just on the news," she replied. "Everyone is suing your dad. Bumfresh has made everyone's bottom go purple."

"*What*?" replied Joe. He turned back to the TV.

"If you are watching out there, son… Come home. Please. I beg you. I need you. I miss you so much…"

Joe reached out and touched the screen. He could feel tears welling in the corners of his eyes. A little hiss of static danced on his fingertips.

"You'd better go to him," said Bob.

"Yeah," said Joe, too shocked to move.

"If you and your dad need anywhere to stay, you are both welcome here," said Bob's mum.

"Yeah, of course," chimed in Bob.

"Thanks so much. I'll tell him," said Joe. "Look, I've gotta go."

"Yeah," said Bob. He opened his arms and gave Joe a hug. Joe couldn't remember the last time anyone had hugged him. It was one thing money couldn't buy. Bob was a brilliant hugger too. He was all squidgy.

"I'll see you later, I suppose," said Joe.

"I'll make a Shepherd's Pie," said Bob's mum with a smile.

"My dad loves Shepherd's Pie," replied Joe.

"I remember," said Bob's mum. "Me and your dad were at school together."

"Really?" asked Joe.

"Yes, he had a bit more hair and a bit less money back then!" she joked.

Joe allowed himself a little laugh. "Thank you so much."

The lift was out of order so Joe raced down the stairs, bouncing off the walls as he did so. He ran out into the car park where Raj was waiting.

"Bumfresh Towers, Raj. And step on it!"

Raj pedalled hard and the trike trundled off down the street. They passed a rival newsagent's shop and Joe clocked the headlines on the papers in racks outside. Dad was on every front page.

BUMFRESH SCANDAL said *The Times*.

BILLIONAIRE SPUD FACING RUIN ran the *Telegraph*.

BUMFRESH IS HARMFUL TO BOTTOMS exclaimed the *Express*.

IS YOUR BOTTOM PURPLE? enquired the *Guardian*.

BUMFRESH PURPLE BOTTOM NIGHT-MARE! screamed the *Mirror*.

QUEEN HAS BABOON'S BUM claimed the *Mail*.

BUM HORROR yelled the *Daily Star*.

POSH SPICE CHANGES HAIRSTYLE announced the *Sun*.

Well, nearly every front page.

"You were right, Raj!" said Joe, as they sped up the high street.

"About what in particular?" replied the

newsagent, as he mopped the sweat from his brow.

"About Bumfresh. It has made everyone's bottom go purple!"

"I told you so! Did you inspect yours?"

So much had happened since Joe had left Raj's shop yesterday afternoon he had completely forgotten. "No."

"Well?" prompted the newsagent.

"Pull over!"

"What?"

"I said, 'pull over'!"

Raj swerved the Rajmobile on to the verge. Joe leaped off, looked over his shoulder and pulled down the back of his trousers a little.

"Well?" asked Raj.

Joe looked down. Two great purple swollen cheeks stared back at him. "It's purple!"

Let's have another look at Raj's graph. If Joe's

bottom was added to it, it would look like this:

In short Joe's bum was **very very very very very
very very very very very very very very very
very very very very very very very very very
very very very very very very very very very
very very very very very very very very very
very very very very very very very very very
very very very very very very very very very**

very very very very very very very very very
very very very very very very very very very
very very very very very very very very...

...*purple*.

Joe pulled up his trousers and jumped back on the Rajmobile. "Let's go!"

As they approached Bumfresh Towers, Joe saw that there were hundreds of journalists and camera crews waiting outside the gates of his house. As they approached, all the cameras turned to them, and hundreds of flashes went off. They were blocking their entrance and Raj had no choice but to stop the trike.

"You are live on Sky News! How do you feel now your father faces financial ruin?"

Joe was too shocked to reply, but still men in raincoats continued to shout questions at him.

"BBC News. Is there going to be a compensation

package for the millions of people around the world whose bums have gone purple?"

"CNN. Do you think your father will face criminal charges?"

Raj cleared his throat. "If I may make a short statement gentlemen."

All the cameras turned to the newsagent and there was hushed silence for a moment.

"At Raj's shop in Bolsover Street I am doing a very special offer on Frazzles. Buy ten packets get one free! For a limited time only."

The journalists all sighed loudly and muttered their annoyance.

Ding ding!

Raj rang the bell on his trike and the sea of reporters parted, to let him and Joe through.

"Thank you so much!" chirped Raj with a smile. "And I have some out of date Lion Bars at half price! Only slightly mouldy!"

26

A Blizzard of Banknotes

As Raj pedalled hard up the long driveway, Joe was shocked to see that there was already a fleet of lorries parked up by the front door. An army of bulky men in leather jackets were carrying out all of his dad's paintings and chandeliers and diamond-encrusted golf clubs. Raj stopped the bike and Joe leaped out of the basket and ran up the huge stone steps. Sapphire was hurrying out in a pair of impossibly high heels, laden with a huge suitcase and numerous handbags.

"Out of my way!" she hissed.

"Where's my dad?" demanded Joe.

"I dunno and I don't care! The idiot has lost all of his money!"

As she ran down the steps the heel of her shoe broke off and she took a tumble. The case crashed on the stone floor and broke open. A blizzard of banknotes swirled into the air. Sapphire began screaming and crying, and as mascara ran down her cheeks she leaped up, trying desperately to catch them. Joe looked back at her with a mixture of anger and pity.

He then raced into the house. It was now completely bare of any belongings. Joe fought past the bailiffs and sprinted up the grand spiral staircase. He passed a couple of burly men making off with hundreds of miles of his Scalextric track. For a millisecond Joe felt a pang of regret, but he carried on running and burst through the door to his dad's bedroom. The room was white and bare, almost serene in its emptiness. Hunched on a bare mattress with his back to the door was his dad, wearing only a vest and a pair of boxer shorts, his fat hairy arms and legs contrasting with his bald head. They had even taken his toupee.

"Dad!" shouted Joe.

"Joe!" Dad turned around. His face was red and raw from crying. "My boy, my boy! You came home."

"I'm sorry I ran away, Dad."

"I am so upset I hurt you with all that business with Lauren. I just wanted to make you happy."

"I know, I know, I forgive you, Dad." Joe sat down next to his father.

"I've lost everything. Everything. Even Sapphire's gone."

"I am not sure she was the one, Dad."

"No?"

"No," replied Joe as he tried not to shake his head too hard.

"No, maybe not," said Dad. "Now we've got no house, no money, no private jet. What are we gonna do, son?"

Joe reached into his trouser pocket and pulled out a cheque. "Dad?"

"Yes, my boy?"

"The other day I was going through my pockets and I found this."

Dad studied it. It was the one he had written his son for his birthday. For two million pounds.

"I never paid it in," said Joe excitedly. "You can have it back. Then you can buy us somewhere to live, and still have loads of money left over."

Dad looked up at his son. Joe wasn't sure if his father was happy or sad.

"Thank you so much, boy. You are a great lad, you really are. But I am sorry to say this cheque is worthless."

"Worthless?" Joe was shocked. "Why?"

"Because I have no money left in my bank

account," explained Dad. "There are so many law suits against me the banks have frozen all my accounts. I'm bankrupt now. If you had paid it in when I gave it to you, we would still have two million pounds."

Joe felt a little bit frightened that somehow he had done the wrong thing. "Are you angry with me, Dad?"

Dad looked at Joe and smiled. "No, I'm pleased you didn't cash it in. All that money never really made us happy, did it?"

"No," said Joe. "In fact it made us sad. And I am sorry too. You brought my homework to school and I shouted at you for embarrassing me. Bob was right, I *have* behaved like a spoiled brat at times."

Dad chuckled. "Well, just a little!"

Joe bumjumped along closer to his dad. He needed a hug.

At that moment two burly bailiffs entered the room. "We've got to take the mattress," announced one.

The Spuds offered no resistance, and stood up to let the men carry the last item out of the room.

Dad leaned over and whispered into his son's ear. "If there's anything you want to grab from your room, boy, I'd do it now."

"I don't need anything, Dad," replied Joe.

"There must be something. Designer shades, a gold watch, your iPod…"

They watched as the two men carried the mattress out of Mr Spud's bedroom. It was now completely bare.

Joe thought for a moment. "There is something," he said. He disappeared out of the room.

Mr Spud moved over to the window. He watched helpless as the leather-jacketed men carried out everything he owned, silver cutlery, crystal vases, antique furniture, everything… and loaded it into the trucks.

In a few moments Joe reappeared.

"Did you manage to grab anything?" asked Dad eagerly.

"Just one thing."

Joe opened his hand and showed his dad the sad little loo-roll rocket.

"But why?" said Dad. He couldn't believe his son had kept the old thing, let alone chosen it as the one thing he wanted to save from the house.

"It's the best thing you ever gave me," said Joe.

Dad's eyes clouded over with tears. "But it's just a loo roll with a bit of another loo roll stuck to it," he spluttered.

"I know," said Joe. "But it was made with

love. And it means more to me than all that expensive stuff you bought me."

Dad shook with uncontrollable emotion, and wrapped his short fat hairy arms around his son. Joe put *his* short, fat, less-hairy arms around his dad. He rested his head on his dad's chest. He felt that it was wet with tears.

"I love you, Dad."

"Ditto… I mean, I love you too, son."

"Dad…?" said Joe tentatively.

"Yes?"

"Do you fancy Shepherd's Pie for tea?"

"More than anything in the world," said Dad with a smile.

Father and son held each other tight.

Finally, Joe had everything he could ever need.

Postscript

So what happened to all the characters in the story?

 Mr Spud liked Bob's mum's Shepherd's Pie so much that he married her. And now they have it every night for their tea.

 Joe and Bob not only stayed best friends – when their parents got married they became stepbrothers too.

 Sapphire got engaged to a Premier League football team.

Raj and Mr Spud began working on a number of ideas together that they hoped would make them zillionaires. The five-fingered Kit Kat. The queen-size Mars Bar (in between king and normal size). Vindaloo-flavoured Polo mints. At time of writing none of these ideas have made them a penny.

No one ever worked out which Grubb was a he and which Grubb was a she. Not even their mum or dad. They were sent to a boot camp in America for juvenile delinquents.

The headmaster, Mr Dust, retired from the school on his hundredth birthday. He now races motorbikes full time.

Miss Spite the history teacher got her job back and gave Joe litter duty every day for the rest of his life.

The unfortunately named teacher Peter Bread changed his name. To Susan Jenkins. Which didn't really help.

Lauren continued her acting career, the only highlight of which was a part in the TV hospital drama *Casualty*. As a dead body.

The headmaster's secretary, Mrs Chubb, never did get out of her chair.

The Queen's bum remained purple. She showed it to everyone in the country when she gave her yearly speech to the nation on Christmas Day, calling it her 'anus horribilis'.

And finally, Mrs Trafe released a best-selling cook book, *101 Recipes with Bat Sick*. Available from HarperCollins.

DISCOVER

www.worldofwalliams.com

Visit Raj's shop and...

*play super-silly games

*collect points for Raj's whoopee surprise

*join the Wallichums and top the leaderboard

*enter amazing competitions to win incredible prizes

And much much more!

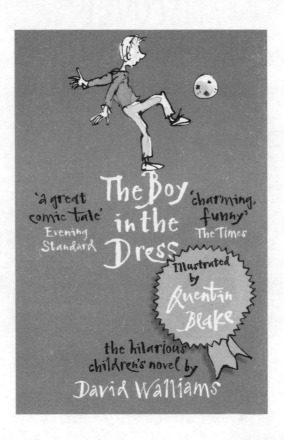

'a great
comic tale'
Evening
Standard

The Boy
in the
Dress

'charming,
funny'
The Times

Illustrated
by
Quentin
Blake

the hilarious
children's novel by
David Walliams

The hilarious first novel by

David Walliams

Available
now in
paperback

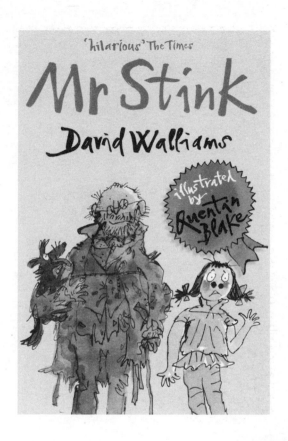

The *even more* hilarious
second novel by

David Walliams

Available
now in
paperback

Out Now!

the screamingly funny new book by

David Walliams

RATBURGER

FREE BURGER from Burt's Burgers*
*Expires 1986